TED TAYLER

CREATURE
DISCOMFORTS

BOOKS

By Ted Tayler

The Freeman Files

Vinci Books

vinci-books.com

Published by Vinci Books Ltd in 2025

1

Paperback ISBN: 9781036704933

Prologue

Sunday, 25 May 2014

GRANT BURNSIDE rarely got out of bed before ten o'clock in the morning.

There was no rush. He had people at his beck and call that rushed around for him.

His long-suffering wife, Maggie, looked after everything at home, and their son, Gary, was supposed to watch everything else.

Youngsters today didn't have the same attention to detail as those Grant knew as a boy. That was why he had to roll out of bed a few minutes after seven. On a Sunday, of all days. Sunday was a day of rest. It was just another day of the week in Grant Burnside's world.

The head of the Burnside clan had recently reached sixty-five years of age. He had spent every day since his teens on the wrong side of the law, and his body bore the evidence to prove it.

His hands were like dinner plates and were scarred and lumpy.

"I'll never play the piano again," he used to tell Maggie.

His wife smiled every time. She knew what to expect if she didn't.

Grant's hands showed the damage they'd caused over the years every bit as much as the pain they'd suffered. The gangster stood a smidgen under six feet tall and was solid with it. He reminded his colleagues of a prizefighter. They saw him as the bloke who came out of the crowd at a funfair to challenge the ex-professional in the boxing booth and knocked seven bells out of him. The word 'hard' didn't cover it.

No way Grant Burnside would ever get caught in a gym working out.

"That's for nancy boys," he'd tell his sons.

Grant kept fit by grafting at home and taking a rare labouring job off the books.

He stripped to the waist in the summer months when doing any manual labour. Nobody queried the three wounds on his torso: two bullet wounds and one stab wound.

Everyone who met one of the Burnside family knew better than to ask.

It was wise never to answer questions about them in case word reached their ears. The punishments for crossing the Burnsides were the stuff of legend in Swindon and the surrounding towns and villages.

Perhaps inevitably, a life defined by violence should end in bloodshed.

Someone planned to put an end to Grant Burnside's life on this sunny Sunday morning

When he got out of bed, Grant Burnside didn't know it was for the last time.

ON THE OTHER side of Swindon, Howard Todd was frightened. He'd left home not long after it got light and threaded his way through the empty streets on the Park South estate. Todd checked every corner to see that nobody lay in wait. He glanced over his shoulder every few seconds to see if he could spot his pursuers.

Todd paused in the doorway of a newsagent. The Sunday newspapers lay by the door in bundles, waiting for someone to arrive to fill the empty spaces in the rack behind him. His sister lived nearby, although it had been a while since he'd visited her, and he wasn't sure of the quickest way to get there from here.

Todd set off after checking in both directions once more. If he was right and this next left turning took him onto Mandy's street, then less than four hundred yards separated him from the shelter of her terraced home. He could hide there until nighttime and persuade Mandy to drive him to Oxford. There was no way he'd survive another twenty-four hours on the streets of Swindon.

The red-brick walls of the narrow alleyway stretched skywards on both sides. Todd whipped his head around when he heard the scrape of a boot against the pavement way behind. Had someone spotted him? He hurried further along the alleyway to escape, and his heart sank when he saw what awaited him.

The row of houses on either side had access to the main road he'd just left for their wheelie bins, bicycles, and tools. There was a twelve-foot red-brick wall with broken glass embedded in the top separating these houses from the gardens of the terraced properties on the street he was desperate to reach.

This alleyway was a dead-end.

Howard Todd swallowed hard. Why couldn't they have called it something else?

He ran at the wall, jumped, and scrambled up as far as possible. It was useless. His eyes darted left and right. There was nothing to use as a weapon. His only hope was to drag a bin from the nearest house and risk having his arms and legs torn to shreds scaling that wall.

It was preferable to what was in store if he got caught.

If only he'd taken the next left turning. His whole life was about making the wrong choices. Howard Todd used to consider the men after him as his friends. They weren't his friends anymore. He'd crossed the line.

For the past eight months, Todd had skimmed a tiny percentage from every contract he'd handled for the Burnside gang. He realised it was stupid, but he wanted the money it brought to finance his own business. Nobody made a fortune working for someone else.

Todd dreamed of a future at the head of his drug dealing business. At this very moment, he just wanted to see tomorrow. The heavy footsteps grew closer. As Todd wrestled with the locked garden gates on the nearest properties, he tried to decide how many of Grant Burnside's thugs there were. Was it two or three? He gave up struggling with the locks and darted across the alleyway to try his luck with the houses on the other side.

Todd didn't dare look back down the alleyway. His ears told him the three men had stopped running. They were walking steadily towards him. He was going nowhere.

"Well, well, Sly Todd. You seem to have taken a wrong

turn. What a pity. You were so close to getting away from us, too."

Gary Burnside himself was at the front of the muscular trio.

"Don't make him feel too bad, Gary," said Denver Drewett. "We've got someone watching Mandy's place. Toddy wouldn't get away from us this time."

Howard Todd looked at the three men blocking the alleyway.

Burnside and Drewett had Vic Hodge riding shotgun. He was another enforcer that Grant Burnside had on his books. All brawn and no brain. Todd knew his options were limited. He could stand still until they made a move on him, or he could fight.

What was he thinking? Three against one. Each was twice as big as he was and well-accustomed to a street fight. His only chance was to run. Vic Hodge was too slow to catch a cold. He might just find a way out if he could get past him.

Howard Todd yelled at the top of his lungs, lowered his head, and ran straight at the lumbering giant. Vic Hodge wasn't used to people running towards him. He was puzzled and wondered what to do next.

As Todd hit Hodge squarely in the gut, the big man stumbled back into the red-brick wall. Todd was almost past Hodge and ready to run for his life. Neither of those three thugs would catch him in a foot race with a few yards head start.

Gary Burnside had spotted Todd eying the numbskull on his right. He calmly allowed the leather cosh to slide into the palm of his hand from his jacket sleeve. As Todd tried to barge through the human barrier, Gary struck Todd twice, once with a straight jab to the kidney and then with a savage blow to the back of the head.

Howard Todd fell against the alleyway wall, and his legs buckled. He sprawled headfirst onto the tarmac, and the lights went out.

"You okay, Vic," asked Gary.

"Yeah, sorry, he surprised me."

Gary waved the cosh under Vic's nose before slipping it into an inside jacket pocket.

"Don't let it happen again, Vic, eh?"

Hodge and Drewett dragged the unconscious Howard Todd to the end of the alleyway. Gary Burnside made a call, and a Mercedes van pulled alongside the four men within minutes. They bundled Todd in the back, got inside, and the van drove away.

The streets of the Park South estate were still empty. While the thugs were dealing with Howard Todd at the alleyway entrance, the odd dog walker and newsagent's staff member strolled or cycled past, but nobody said a word. They well knew the Mercedes van across the town.

Drewett and Hodge sat in the back with their prisoner while Gary sat in the cab with the driver.

"You took your time, son," said Grant Burnside. "at least me getting out of bed at this ungodly hour hasn't been a waste of time."

After a ten-minute drive, Grant brought the van to a halt outside a row of commercial units on the Cheney Manor Industrial Estate. Gary jumped out and went inside. Grant watched the roller door sliding up to give them access in his rear-view mirror. He reversed inside and killed the engine.

"Nice and quiet out here this morning," said Grant. "We won't get disturbed. Why don't you let the lads have fun while we get ourselves a mug of tea? Nothing permanent, you understand."

"Okay, Dad," said Gary. He opened the rear doors, and Drewett and Hodge frogmarched Howard Todd inside the unit. Gary closed the roller door.

"There's plenty of heavy-duty plastic sheeting over there in the corner," he told the lads, "don't get the floor dirty. The boss said you could take the first crack. To get him used to real pain. It might make what's coming not so hard to bear."

Howard Todd's head was clearing. They must have bound him, hand, and foot, inside the Mercedes. Hodge held him upright while Drewett laid light blue sheeting on the floor in the centre of the unit. Todd wondered why.

Hodge shoved him to the ground. Todd fell face first and knew his nose had broken from the first jolt of pain. He soon forgot his nose as Drewett and Hodge took turns kicking and punching him. After several minutes, he was so dazed and numb that he could only lie watching the light blue sheeting turning red. Todd blacked out again.

"A nice cuppa that was," said Grant Burnside, smacking his lips. "No biscuits, though. What a pity. Right, the lads have had their fun. Let's get in there and see what's what."

When Howard Todd awoke for the second time, he found himself sitting on a chair. His ankles were firmly secured to the front legs, and his hands were still tied behind his back. His eyes were closed, but he could see the person walking towards him when he raised his head.

Grant strolled across to where Howard Todd sat. The gangster's sheer presence filled the room. A fluorescent tube flickered above Todd's head. The frightened man shrank back in the chair as if to give Grant Burnside room to breathe.

"Welcome back, Howard," said Grant. "You led us a merry dance. Fair play to you. I don't know why you wore yourself out running, though, because we would always catch up with you, eventually. I can't abide employees who think they can steal from their bosses and get away with it. You got paid well for the work you were doing. Let me ask you something. One hundred and eleven? Does that number mean anything to you, Toddy?"

Howard tried to speak but could only cough as pain racked his bruised and battered body.

"That was the number of occasions you profited from a score that should have come to me. I ask you—over one hundred times in just eight months. I wasn't great at school, but even I could work out that you cheated me every other day. What possessed you? Somebody was bound to notice."

Todd sensed another person edging closer to him from his left.

"Cat got your tongue?" Gary whispered in his ear, "maybe this will help."

Todd heard a swishing sound through the air. The next sound he heard was someone screaming. It was him.

Gary had smashed his left knee with a baseball bat. The pain was excruciating.

"You know what happens to people who cross us," said Gary. "Aren't you going to beg for your life, you ungrateful little worm?"

Todd was ready for the next blow. He groaned, bit his tongue and tried everything to stop himself from caving in as the baseball bat crunched into his right knee.

"I fear my running days may be over," he growled as blood seeped from his mouth and a red bubble of snot escaped his nose.

Grant Burnside elbowed Gary out of the way.

"That's enough, Gary," he snarled. "I want him to pay for every one of those one hundred and eleven missing bags. He hasn't got enough body parts to even the score. Fetch me more plastic sheeting and the tools."

Howard Todd realised that things were going to get deadly serious.

He managed a dry laugh at his ludicrous thought.

"Oh, you think it's funny?" snarled Gary.

Todd raised his head to stare into the eyes of his tormentor.

"You'll never be more than a pawn while the king is still in the game. Don't you get fed up with taking orders from him day after day? At least I tried to break the shackles to run a business I could call my own."

"Yeah," scoffed Gary, "look how well that's turned out for you."

Dumb and Dumber had finished spreading extra plastic sheeting around the chair, and Grant Burnside had everything he required.

Howard Todd looked at the bolt cutters, nail-gun, and machete lined up, ready for action.

He shrugged his shoulders and resigned himself to his fate.

"Get on with it," he said. "You can't blame a bloke for trying."

Chapter One

THE MERCEDES VAN drove out of the warehouse one hour later. Denver Drewett and Vic Hodge stayed behind to carry out the clean-up. Gary Burnside and his father had a delivery to make. The mortal remains of Howard Todd were on their way to a farm near Blunsdon. Grant took the A419 road towards Cricklade and turned off onto the minor road that led to the farm.

Thirty-five minutes later, they parked outside an outbuilding. It was a trip they had made frequently when someone stepped out of line, and an example made. Fergus McHugh's family had farmed here for three generations. Although pig farming had significantly contributed to the family income for many decades, Fergus accepted the inevitability of the need to diversify.

Grant Burnside had bumped into Fergus McHugh in a pub in Purton four years ago. He remembered the conversation very well. Grant had always lived in town, so his impression of pigs was false. He thought they were filthy animals, and Grant stood further along the bar from Fergus to avoid the stench. The farmer had told him pigs were the cleanest animals in the farmyard. They wallowed in mud to cool themselves because they didn't have sweat glands.

Grant asked Fergus how he felt about slaughtering a proportion of his stock every winter. The elderly farmer shrugged and replied that it was part of pig farming. But, because it was vital, his father had reduced the disposal of things with zero marketable value to a fine art. Fergus had adopted the same system when he inherited the farm after his father died.

Grant thought this disposal system sounded promising and bought Fergus another pint. He moved closer and invited Fergus to tell him more.

"Lye is a corrosive alkali found in household cleaners," the farmer told him. "Most people realise acids are caustic, but few realise that their chemical opposites can be just as destructive. Lye's toxicity at the highest can be super toxic."

"So, that's what you use then," asked Grant, "It works better than a lime-pit such as the ones you see in the films, does it?"

"Never believe what those filmmakers tell you," Fergus had said. "It takes less than seven drops in an oral dose, a mere taste, to be lethal to a seventy-kilogram human being. A single taste of lye causes third-degree burns on the mouth and the tube connecting the throat to the stomach. If a sufficiently large dose of lye gets swallowed, the alkali can cause perforations in the stomach, leading to death."

"I admit it sounds like a gruesome way of killing some-one," Grant said, taking a swig of his pint. "But how do you persuade someone to drink the stuff? If they did, you've still got a body on your hands. How do a few drops of this lye stuff help to get rid of the bits of pig you've got left?"

Fergus McHugh explained the process.

"Under high heat and pressure, lye turns corrosive enough to disintegrate fat, bones, and skin. In three hours, my lye solution, heated to three hundred degrees Fahrenheit, dissolves an entire body into an oily brown liquid."

"Just say, for argument's sake, I had something I wanted to dispose of," Grant had asked. "Could you do it for the right price?"

Fergus McHugh had thought for a moment and then nodded.

"The equipment stands idle most of the time. If you see me right financially, I don't see a problem. After the process is over, I pour the oily liquid down the drain."

Grant decided to immediately change their method of disposing of bodies. Before that chance meeting in the pub, he, and his father before him, buried any corpses in nearby woods or dumped them in sewers or the river. That method was risky. Dead bodies could be discovered and the evidence they contained used against them. Fergus McHugh's operation offered a perfect solution.

Grant had called yesterday to tell Fergus McHugh that a van would arrive this morning. Fergus's job was to make sure he had enough stock whenever someone from the Burnside gang delivered a package to be able to carry out his side of the bargain.

Grant and his son entered the outbuilding and loaded Todd's remains into the large steel container in the centre of the room. Grant placed an envelope filled with the cash payment on a nearby table.

As they drove out of the yard, Grant knew Fergus would appear from inside the farmhouse. Once inside the outbuilding, the elderly farmer put on protective gloves and a gas mask. He then boiled the package in the lye solution for eight hours until only the teeth, and the nails remained.

Fergus destroyed those last pieces of evidence by burning them with petrol in a wood near the farm boundary.

Fergus and Grant hadn't met in person since that night four years earlier. The occasional phone call was the only link between them. Nobody questioned why an unmarked van appeared in the farmyard to make a delivery. Why should they?

"That was money well spent," said Grant as they returned to the Cheney Manor Industrial Estate to collect Denver and Vic, the clean-up crew,

"Sly Todd has disappeared for good," said Gary. "There's no danger of us getting linked to anything. We'll do what we always do, make sure the right people know why he's not around. It will send a clear message not to cross us."

"What are you doing later?" asked Grant, "this work has made me hungry. Once we've dropped off your gophers, why don't we collect the girls and go for a Sunday lunch?"

Gary wasn't sure his stomach was stable enough to tuck into a roast dinner after this morning's events. But he knew his father didn't want to hear that, so he called Kirstin and told her to get ready.

"Do you want me to call Maggie?" asked Kirstin, "to warn her Grant will expect her to be ready to jump to it as soon as he reaches home?"

"Good idea," said Gary, "forewarned is forearmed. I'll see you within the hour. I need to shower and change before we go out."

Denver and Vic were still inside the warehouse unit when Grant backed the Mercedes van up to the roller door.

Gary went inside to check on their progress. He needn't have worried. The heavy-duty plastic sheeting had been hosed down and stacked away in the corner. The unit floor bore no visual evidence of what had occurred two hours earlier.

"Did you clean the tools, too?" he asked.

Denver Drewett nodded.

"They're locked in the cabinet, ready for use whenever needed," he replied.

"Come on then," said Gary. "We'll drop you two home, and then we can enjoy what's left of Sunday."

As the three men walked towards the exit, they heard a crack.

"What the heck was that?" asked Vic.

"It sounded like a car backfiring," said Denver.

Gary thought it sounded more like a gunshot, but it couldn't be, not in the middle of nowhere.

Once they were outside, Denver and Vic climbed into the back of the van, and Gary locked the unit door. He looked around the various industrial units, but nobody was working, and no other vehicles were in sight.

"What was that loud bang just now, Dad?" Gary asked as he prepared to swing himself into the passenger seat of the truck's cab.

The neat hole in the windscreen caught his attention first, and when he turned his head to the right, Gary saw what remained of his dead father's face.

Gary fell back out of the cab, collapsed to his knees and threw up.

Denver Drewett and Vic Hodge banged on the sides in the back of the truck, wanting to know what had happened. When he recovered, Gary let them out.

"Who would have wanted to shoot Grant?" asked Drewett.

Vic Hodge didn't say a word. He knew Denver was brighter than him. But be fair. Even Vic knew there was a list as long as your arm of people who wanted Grant Burnside dead.

Vic thought the question should be—who dared to do it? There wouldn't be many names on *that* list.

"What do you want us to do, Gary?" he asked.

"We can't leave him there," said Denver.

"Just shut it for a minute, will you?" yelled Gary, "I need to think."

Gary realised there was no way to cover this up. He had to call the police, even if it was the last thing he wanted to do.

Gary looked at the windscreen again. Where had the shot come from? Dad wouldn't have sat there and let a gunman walk up to the van and open fire. It had to be a rifle with a large calibre bullet to make that mess. Could there have been a sniper lying on the roof of one of the other warehouse units? Any gunman would be long gone by now. How the heck did they know Grant was going to be here this morning? It was a Sunday, and Dad never worked on a Sunday. Gary was desperately trying to think who could have fired the shot that ended his father's life.

"Are we certain that everything connecting us to Howard Todd has gone from inside that warehouse?" he asked.

"Forensics might find something, Gary," said Denver. "You need to get hold of Iverson. He'll know what to do."

Gary made the call, and Patrick Iverson drove into the yard twenty minutes later. He'd been the Burnside family solicitor for half a century. What he didn't know about the family's crooked dealings and punishment beatings wasn't worth knowing.

His legal representation didn't come cheap, but Grant's father, George, had argued that if Iverson kept him out of prison, it was worth every penny. So Iverson was suited and booted, as always, and parked his Jaguar far away from the Mercedes.

Vic Hodge wondered whether he ever went out without wearing a suit and tie.

"What happened?" asked Iverson, approaching the van but keeping his distance from the cab.

"Dad and I had business to attend to," said Gary. "We visited here earlier with these two and carried out the first phase. Then we drove out Blunsdon way, finished our business, and returned. I went inside to collect Vic and Denver, and someone shot Dad."

"Don't tell me what the business was," said Iverson. "I don't want to know. Is there anything incriminating in the van?"

"I'll check the cab," said Gary, swallowing hard. "I don't think Dad had a weapon of any kind. There might be blood on the floor in the back."

Patrick Iverson shuddered.

"What about inside the warehouse?"

"We cleaned it well, Mr Iverson," said Vic Hodge.

"Yeah, it's clean, but it might not be good enough to fool forensics," added Denver Drewett.

"That's okay," said Iverson, "check the van's rear compartment. If you have bleach available, spread it liberally on any affected areas. I'll think up a plausible explanation. As for the unit, the police will need to get a search warrant. There's nothing to suggest it's connected to the killing. If nobody saw you earlier, you can say the shooting occurred as soon as you arrived. You didn't have time to work inside before rushing outside to help Grant. I know what you want to do, Gary, but please don't rush to the other units searching for clues. Leave that to the police. We need to act fast. We can't delay notifying the authorities for much longer."

Gary checked the glove compartment and the floor of the cab. As he had thought, there weren't any hidden weapons. The paperwork for the vehicle was in order—nothing to fear there. Vic and Denver checked inside the van. Because they'd done a grand job of wrapping Howard Todd's body parts, there were only a few stains that needed a quick scrub with bleach from the warehouse unit toilet. Patrick Iverson took a quick look.

"Okay, Gary, make the call," he said. "When they ask what time I arrived, tell them you rang me immediately after you made the emergency call, and I was driving towards the Manor."

Iverson turned to the others and said, "Leave as much talking to me as possible, do you understand?"

Denver and Vic nodded.

Ten minutes later, the four men heard sirens in the distance.

Monday, 26 May 2014

GRANT BURNSIDE'S murder made headlines in every regional newspaper and on local TV.

Gary Burnside watched the news reports at home with his wife, Kirstin. Their children had gone to primary school despite the death of their grandfather.

"Is your Mum going to be okay, Gary," asked Kirstin, "should we be with her?"

"My sister Kerry's at home, and Henry and Joseph said they'd drop by."

Kirstin decided not to say another word. Maggie wouldn't get a slap for a word spoken out of turn from either of those three. Grant had been her tormentor for forty years. So, in her world, Maggie was already okay. Kirstin leaned into her husband's shoulder and listened to the reporter on screen.

"On two occasions in the past three years, a smiling Grant Burnside walked from court a free man. In 2010, a jury cleared him of the murder of Spencer Curtis. The forty-four-year-old gang member was found stabbed to death in the back of his car near Wroughton in 2009. Burnside's background as a hardened criminal with convictions for assault, robbery, firearms, and drugs was not revealed to the jury at the Crown Court in Chippenham. Burnside served four years for robbery in 1977, was sentenced to a further five for an armed raid in 1983, and got six years for drug dealing in 1996. The court heard that Burnside abducted Curtis and drove him to land near a golf club on the outskirts of Calne. The next morning, police found Curtis's mutilated body in the back of his car after receiving an anonymous phone call. Despite the prosecution's claims, the jury found Burnside not guilty. The Burnside family solicitor, Patrick Iverson, applauded the verdict and said switching the trial from Swindon to Chippenham had given his client a better chance of a fair trial. A crowd of twenty Burnside family members cheered his comments to our reporter. Police believed that Curtis's murder resulted from a drug deal that went wrong. Spencer Curtis's widow, Jasmine, had to identify her husband's body after returning from a holiday in the Maldives. Her comment after the trial was - 'Somebody killed my darling, Spence. If it wasn't Burnside, who else could it be?' Last year, Blake Dixon died before giving evidence against one of Grant Burnside's sons. Grant Burnside was charged with blasting Dixon in the chest at point-blank range with a sawn-off shotgun. The shooting happened in the presence of at least four witnesses at a snooker club in Swindon. The police couldn't find anyone to stand up in court and say what they witnessed. Blake Dixon was a thirty-seven-year-old entrepreneur well-known on the nightclub circuit as a drug dealer. Yet again, Burnside walked from court with a huge grin. Detective Inspector Theo Hickerton from Gablecross Police Station told me that Grant Burnside believed he was invincible. He intimidated potential witnesses, threatened their families, and severely punished anyone who crossed him. Grant made too many enemies. It was only a matter of time before someone took care of him."

"Who did it, Gary," asked Kirstin, "do you know?"

"Not a clue, sweetheart," said Gary, "but he's a dead man walking."

Chapter Two

Friday, 15 June 2018

GUS DROVE HOME from work to Urchfont at lunchtime and grabbed a quick sandwich and a cup of coffee before walking up the lane to Bert Penman's house. The funerals of six of his old friend's close family members were taking place today, many miles away in Saskatchewan, Canada.

It was essential to put everything else to one side on days like today. Words weren't always necessary but being there was vital.

Gus knocked on Bert's front door and heard him call out.

"It's open."

Gus found Bert sitting in a comfortable chair, chatting with Irene North and Clemency Bentham in the living room. The two ladies had kept Bert company since mid-morning. The Reverend's idea had been to keep Bert occupied so he didn't dwell too much on the awfulness. Gus looked at the faces that turned towards him as he entered.

There was little chance of that, as Gus suspected. To lose a son and daughter-in-law in a traffic accident was bad enough. Bert's granddaughter, her husband, and two children had also died after an express train obliterated their vehicle on a level crossing.

Clemency Bentham nudged Irene North. The older lady was nodding off in the chair. It was time to let the afternoon shift take over.

"We'll leave you two gentlemen alone," said Clemency. "I'll drop in to see you later, Bert."

"Thank you, Reverend," said Bert. "Irene, don't forget to pick up those vegetables I put by for you. They're on the kitchen table."

"You do too much for me, Bertie," said Irene, kissing the retired butcher on the forehead. "Thank you."

"We grow more on our allotments than we can eat ourselves, don't we, Mr Freeman?" said Bert. "They'd only go to waste if I didn't give produce to those whose need is greater than mine."

Irene North shuffled off to the kitchen.

"How am I going to manage this lot?" she cried when she saw the produce piled on the large wooden table.

"There should be a trug by the back door, Irene," called Bert. "Fill it with as much as you can carry, and let me have it back when you're ready."

Gus could see the puzzlement on Clemency's face.

"It's a shallow oblong basket made from strips of wood. They've been around for centuries."

"Ah, I see," said the Reverend, "I learn something every time I visit him."

"One new fact every day is the high road to success," said Gus, "or so I learned at school."

"That trug was my mother's," said Bert, "so you're

not far wrong, Mr Freeman. That old basket has certainly seen service. They made things to last in those days."

Irene North returned from the kitchen with her basket filled with broad beans, cabbages, lettuces, spring onions and a dozen new potatoes.

"We'll be off then," said Clemency. Gus watched the pair negotiate the front garden path and reach the safety of the village street.

"Peace at last," sighed Bert. "I've drunk too many cups of tea today. Both of them mean well, but now that you're here, we can do better. Did you walk over from the bungalow, Mr Freeman?"

Gus nodded.

"Fetch us a flagon of cider from the kitchen," Bert continued. "I'll get two glasses from the cabinet, and you can tell me what you've been up to this week."

Gus gave Bert a summary of the Mark Malone murder case. Then they spent the rest of the afternoon putting the world to rights, polishing off a second two litres of cider. Gus took the empty cider bottles and the glasses through to the kitchen. The old clock on the wall showed a quarter to four.

The few remaining members of Bert's family would breakfast now if they could face it. His daughter, Margaret, and her family had flown from New Zealand to grieve with Brett, the sole survivor from the Canadian branch of the Penman family.

Clemency had told Gus that Margaret planned to visit the UK before returning home. Her nephew, Brett, might accompany her, and he was considering emigrating as he had nothing to hold him in Canada any longer. His veterinary skills would soon find him a job, especially in Wiltshire.

There seemed to be more animals than people in these parts some days.

"What do you plan to do until the Reverend gets back?" asked Gus when he walked back into the living room.

Gus found Bert standing by the front door with his walking stick.

"With the prospect of a warm summer evening ahead, I reckon we should walk along the lane to the allotments, Mr Freeman," said Bert. "I can get two hours of work done before the Reverend returns to hold my hand."

"We both need to put work in, Bert," sighed Gus, "I've not had the time to spare."

"There's always something that needs attention, even in July," said Bert as they made their way slowly along the lane. "I want to sow my main crop of carrots this weekend. Last year, I remember you were getting on with your winter cabbage and leek. What were you thinking of planting this year?"

"Bert, I haven't given it a thought," said Gus as they left the lane and walked through the gateway to the field of allotments. "Somewhere in my shed is a scribbled set of notes I made when you told me what I should do and when. Unless I dig it out each year at the right time, it's disastrous. I check what you've done during the week while I'm at work and try to match it. If you're not here to chastise me for stinting on my hoeing and watering, this patch will soon fall into disrepair."

"Recent events show that I can't count on being around forever, Mr Freeman," said Bert. He leaned on his stick and gazed towards the old church that had stood there for eight hundred years.

"What time is it in Canada, Mr Freeman?" he asked.

"Lunchtime," said Gus. "Come and sit, Bert. We can talk, or you can sit while I work."

"I think I'll spend time in St Michael's," said Bert, "on my own, if you don't mind. I'll leave you to get on with your chores and wander home in plenty of time to save the Reverend standing on my doorstep like a lost soul. Thank you for passing the afternoon with me. It's much appreciated."

"What are friends for?" said Gus.

Bert Penman left him and soon disappeared inside the old church.

Gus knew the pain of losing loved ones, but he had never felt the need to pray or seek solace from talking with someone such as Clemency Bentham. Whatever it took to get Bert Penman through to the other side of this tragedy, Gus hoped it worked.

After a few minutes of searching for those scribbled notes without success, Gus got on with hoeing and watering. Time slipped past. When he next looked towards the church clock, it was already a quarter past seven. Bert had left for home over an hour ago. Clemency Bentham was with him now, and he was in safe hands.

Gus put his tools away in the shed, locked up, and returned to the bungalow.

Time to feed the inner man. While his evening meal was cooked, he listened to the tortured tones of Janis Joplin.

Gus glanced at his watch. Suzie Ferris would be here in the next half hour. He had time to shower and change into his glad rags. He and Suzie were joining the Crime Review Team members at the Waggon & Horses for a celebratory drink.

Gus was deciding which shirt to wear when he heard the key in the door. It was a sound he'd been used to when Tess was alive. Neither worked what people used to call regular hours. So, hearing a key in the door at odd times was a common occurrence for both.

Gus had grown accustomed to living alone in the last three years, but times had changed.

"Are you decent?" called Suzie.

"When it's appropriate," he replied as he walked into the hallway from the bedroom.

"Mmm," said Suzie, "is that what you're wearing?"

"I thought it might be an option," said Gus.

"Think again," said Suzie, "let's get in the bedroom and see what else you have available."

"We don't have time if we're meeting the others at half-past nine."

"Easy, tiger. I need to put my things in your wardrobe, anyway."

Gus finally noticed Suzie's garment holder on her shoulder, holding it casually with a thumb through the loop. Suzie swung it around and folded it over her arm.

"Lead on," she said.

Five minutes later, Gus was resplendent in a crisp white shirt, and his clothes had squeezed further along the rail to make room for more items Suzie had transferred from home.

"Have your parents noticed anything unusual in your behaviour of late?" Gus asked as he closed the front door behind them.

"My parents like you, Gus, don't forget," said Suzie. "They'll be sad to see me go when I do. We'll take my car. As much as I enjoy recovering from a hangover on a Saturday morning ride, you deserve a drink after everything that's happened this week."

Neatly done, thought Gus. Perhaps I'm still on probation.

At least he could dismiss thoughts of what Bert Penman was suffering. Of course, it helped that they were celebrating ACC Dominic Culverhouse's fall from a great height. Nobody would shed tears over that creep tonight.

The scene that greeted them at The Waggon & Horses was familiar. Cars littered the grass verges on either side of the road because the car park was full. Suzie squeezed her VW Golf into a parking space his old Ford Focus would have refused to attempt. The others were inside the crowded bar.

"A disco tonight in the Stable bar, guv," said Neil Davis once he spotted his boss working his way through the crowd. "The band cried off at the last minute."

"We must be thankful for small mercies, Neil," said Gus. He scanned the bar for signs of the others.

"We're in the corner of the bar beyond the restaurant, guv," said Neil. "Give me your order, and I'll bring them through. Amelia's holding two seats in there for you."

"Oh, PC Cranston has joined us, has she?" said Gus, "I'll have a pint of lager."

"A slimline tonic with ice and lemon for me, Neil, thanks," said Suzie. "I'm a designated driver."

Neil must have bought the bar staff a drink earlier because both dashed to serve him. That never happened when Gus was waiting,

"Melody wasn't feeling up to it, guv," said Neil when he returned with the drinks, "I bumped into Amelia in town when I was shopping, and she was at a loose end. I hope you don't mind. She's an honorary CRT member after working on my Dad's case and DI Ferris's kidnapping."

"How's Alex?" asked Gus.

"Quiet, guv," said Neil, "but he looks more with it than he did when you sent him home."

"Small steps, Neil," said Gus, "We mustn't rush him. I know I can rely on you and Lydia to stop him from back-sliding."

"It will be good to get the A-Team back together, guv," said Neil, "I don't suppose you know what we're in for next week? Any news from London Road about a new case?"

"I didn't ask, Neil," said Gus. "I made sure the paper-work relating to the Malone case got to the ACC before he left for the weekend and hoped it would sustain his good mood until Monday. Geoff Mercer was like a dog with two tails. Nailing Culverhouse was the icing on the cake after clearing another cold case."

Neil led the way, and they were soon in the relative quiet of the corner of the bar.

"Evening, guv," came a chorus of voices. Gus saw Lydia Logan Barre sitting with Alex Hardy.

Lydia looked stunning. Alex looked nervous.

"Suzie," called Amelia Cranston, "you two can sit here by Neil and me."

Suzie glanced towards Gus. He shrugged what he hoped amounted to a 'whatever' response.

"I feel the odd one out," said the young man sitting with Luke Sherman, "I'm not a policeman."

"Hello," said Gus, "you must be Nicky. It's good to meet you. Don't worry. I've told this lot before to dispense with formalities on social occasions, but they find it hard to change the habits of a lifetime. It's Gus for everyone tonight."

"How was your afternoon, guv, Gus?" asked Luke.

"Bert Penman and I drank rough cider and discussed

everything under the sun to stop him thinking of his family."

"Did it work?" asked Lydia.

"I thought it had until we reached the allotments. Bert went inside the church for a while. That place holds a host of memories for him. I can't remember where he told me he and Cora got married, but they spent all their married life in Urchfont. No doubt his children went there for their christening, Sunday School, and confirmation classes."

"What a dreadful thing to have happened," said Nicky, "Luke told me last night."

"I suggest we take a moment to reflect on how fragile life can be," said Gus.

He sat beside Suzie, and there was a brief lull in the conversation. Even the chirpy Amelia Cranston got the message,

"How do you rate Kenneth Truelove's chances, guv?" asked Neil.

"I think he's dreading getting asked to continue as Acting Chief Constable for the foreseeable future," said Gus.

"The Police and Crime Commissioner can't have enjoyed the frequent changes in the top job in the past three months. Even if they were unavoidable," said Alex. "My bet is he'll want a period of stability, and Truelove's a safe pair of hands who would be at Devizes for another year, anyway. Twelve months gives the PCC time to find the right man or woman for the job."

"I think you're right, Alex," said Gus, "but the ACC wants to get out as soon as possible. He fears his wife's reaction to his accepting the role far more than telling the PCC to shove it."

"We should continue to give him our total support,

regardless," said Neil. "The CRT wouldn't exist if it weren't for him. The ACC convinced the top brass to let him get Gus out of retirement and then fought Sandra Plunkett's attempts to shut us down."

"I think we've repaid his trust in us so far," said Alex. "Even though I didn't work on the latest case, our success rate is impressive. As long as we keep delivering positive results, we should survive whoever's in charge."

"I guess Lydia told you we're adding another body to the team from July?" asked Gus.

"Yes," said Alex, "actually, she mentioned Blessing's name before Geoff Mercer learned that her family was moving south to Bath."

"Blessing impressed me when we met in Cirencester," said Lydia. "She's young and raw, but that's no bad thing. She's eager to learn."

Gus caught the look she gave him. Did Lydia expect him to say something?

"Geoff Mercer didn't offer me an opportunity to vet the original members of my team," he said. "It's been tough, but considering he dumped you three on me, I reckon I deserve a medal for knocking you into shape so quickly."

"I was lucky to be in the right place at the right time," said Luke. "I didn't give it a second thought when DS Mercer asked if I'd fill in for Neil when he went on special assignment."

"It was me who was lucky," said Gus. "I would have been a dead man if you hadn't been right behind me that morning when Eron Dushka tried to kill me."

"I think Alex hit the nail on the head," said Suzie, "positive results breed confidence. When everyone on the team performs at a high level, especially with the example given by the person at the helm, nobody will threaten what you're doing. They'd be fools to change a winning team."

"We started like a Championship side," said Neil, "with high hopes and ambitions."

"Here we go," said Gus, "We can always rely on Neil to use a football analogy."

"Yes, Gus," said Neil. "Now, we're a Premiership club with aspirations of a Champions League spot. Our squad needs strengthening. Alex and DC Umeh will be with us from the beginning of July. Who knows whether there will be further summer signings?"

"You are funny, Neil," gushed Amelia.

Gus groaned. Suzie dug him in the ribs.

"Who's ready for another drink?" asked Nicky.

"We've got a tab running behind the bar," said Neil, "it's under the name of Freeman."

"Cheeky beggar," said Gus.

"That's what we did last time, Gus," said Alex, "Neil thought it made sense."

"Trust me to be on soft drinks when you're paying, Gus," said Suzie.

"You can have a glass of wine when we get home," he replied. That earned him another dig in the ribs.

The drinks and banter flowed more readily as the night progressed. Finally, Gus settled the bar bill on his return from a trip to the Gents just as the landlord asked if the remaining stragglers didn't have their own homes.

"That's our signal to leave," said Suzie. "Thanks for a great evening. I'm sure I'll bump into many of you at London Road."

"Can we give anyone a lift?" asked Nicky.

"No, thanks," said Amelia, "Neil booked us a taxi. It should be outside in the lane."

"We'll get off then, Gus," said Luke, "see you on Monday."

"Likewise," said Lydia, "I'll drop Alex off on my way home to Chippenham."

"Not long now, Alex," said Gus, shaking his colleague's hand. "Keep up the excellent work. We look forward to seeing you back with us in a fortnight."

"Thanks, guv. I can't wait," said Alex. He and Lydia made their way out of the bar through the empty restaurant. Gus and Suzie followed behind.

"Alex's walking's slightly improved," Gus whispered. "He might dispense with the stick by the time he rejoins the team."

"Look," said Suzie as they reached the outer door. Neil and Amelia stood on the grass verge, waiting for their taxi.

"What did I miss?" asked Gus, "I was watching Lydia reverse out of that parking space. She travels faster in reverse than I do going forwards when I don't know the road."

"She's all over Neil like a rash," said Suzie, "poor Melody. It's not right."

"Geoff warned me she had a reputation," said Gus. "He's got her on the shortlist to join the team. I'm all for diversity, and the girl has the right qualities from what I've seen. However, I fear she'll prove more trouble than she's worth."

"Geoff's a good man," said Suzie as they reached her car. "He won't force anyone on you if you explain your reasoning."

"Did I put my foot in it earlier?" asked Gus when they sat inside the car.

"It's no secret we are together," said Suzie. "Luke saw us

in the back of the car when he drove us home from Leek Wootton."

"You were all over *me* like a rash that night," laughed Gus, "it's catching."

"Aren't you concerned about Neil's behaviour?"

"He's a grown man. I won't interfere in his private life, and I'd hope he'd keep his nose out of mine. My only concern is how he performs within the Crime Review Team. If it affects his work, then it becomes an issue. You saw how I dealt with Alex. Neil would suffer the same fate. He'd be off the team until he could guarantee one hundred per cent focus one hundred per cent of the time. As for Amelia Cranston, I won't entertain adding her name to our merry band if she's a divisive influence."

"That's fair enough," said Suzie. "When you mentioned the glass of wine later, Amelia worried me. I'm happy that the team knows that we're spending time together, but Amelia doesn't know the meaning of the word secret. So she'll spread the rumour at London Road on Monday morning that we're living together."

"You'll see her before I do," said Gus, "put her straight."

Suzie started the car.

"If she talks, she talks," she said. "I spend a good deal of time with you at the bungalow. Let's get back there. You can pour me a large red wine and convince me you want me to take the last step."

Monday, 18 June 2018

"ANOTHER DAY OF ANTICIPATION, GUV," said Neil Davis when Gus Freeman strolled through the lift doors at five minutes to nine.

"*Plus ca change, plus c'est la meme chose*," replied Gus.

"If you say so, guv. We never did Italian at school. The teachers struggled to get us to speak English, let alone a foreign language. What did it mean?"

"It was French, Neil, which means the more things change, the more they stay the same. So despite three attempts at roadworks to improve the situation between here and Devizes, I'm convinced I take longer every Monday to reach the Old Police Station."

"Perhaps the novelty has worn off, guv," said Luke Sherman, who had followed Gus upstairs in the lift. "When you first came out of retirement, you were keen and enthusiastic. After half a dozen cases that reminded you of the pain and suffering certain individuals inflict on others, you're wondering why you bothered. There's always another case, and it's hard not to believe the message coming back from the uniformed officers at the sharp end who say we're fighting a losing battle."

"Come on, Lydia," said Gus, "where are you? I need your beaming smile and a light-hearted quip about something trivial. This conversation is too dark and dismal for me on Monday."

Luke and Neil disappeared into the restroom. Gus heard the Gaggia fire up above the low hum of conversation. Maybe they were discussing the events of Friday night.

As far as Gus could tell, the get-together had achieved its purpose of a team celebration. The first they'd had since they solved Daphne Tolliver's murder. On that level, it was a success. Gus wasn't a fan of spending excessive time with his work colleagues at social events. He believed in maintaining a discreet distance between himself and his team. It was how senior detectives in Salisbury had operated, and he saw no good reason to change.

As the clock on the wall in front of him flicked round to nine o'clock, the lift doors opened and in breezed Lydia Logan Barre. An orange bandana attempted to control her unruly mop of hair. Her latest version of conservative office wear to pacify Gus was a crisp, white shirt over the tight black leather skirt.

Gus closed his eyes. With luck, they wouldn't need to drive anywhere today to interview members of the public. Lydia's short skirt emphasised her impressive pair of legs, and in the few months she'd worked with him, Gus knew that at least one interviewee had almost had a heart attack when the young woman entered the room. Although, that could have been his guilty conscience.

"Gosh, I was nearly late," she said, "Alex forgot to set the alarm. I told him he couldn't afford to be late when he started work again. Are the boys in the restroom?"

Gus nodded.

"I'll bring your coffee back, guv," she said as she rocked towards the door on her four-inch heels.

Lydia returned a few minutes later, with Luke and Neil trailing behind. She placed Gus's black, no sugar coffee beside his keyboard and slipped a Bourbon biscuit alongside.

"In my day, it was an apple for the teacher," he said, "but a chocolate Bourbon is acceptable. Is this to mark a special occasion?"

"It was my birthday yesterday, but Alex and I were too busy to bake a cake," Lydia replied.

"Oh, you never mentioned that on Friday night," said Neil. "Happy Birthday."

"Ditto," said Luke, "let me see. You were twenty-five, am I right?"

"Yeah, another milepost on the road to thirty," Lydia said grimly.

"You make thirty sound as if it's the start of old age," said Gus.

"Being in your sixties hasn't harmed your chances, guv," said Neil.

"Steady on, DS Davis. There's a time and place, you know."

"Sorry, guv," said Neil.

Gus's phone rang. The bell saved him.

"Freeman speaking. How may I help?"

It was Kenneth Truelove, with the usual Monday morning request for his attendance at a meeting.

"I'll be with you in forty-five minutes, Sir," Gus said.

Lydia could hear the ACC chuntering as Gus replaced the phone.

"He was still speaking, guv,"

"He thought I should be able to drive to London Road in thirty minutes. That man does not understand how bad the roads are in this county. He needs to stop staring out his window and get out more."

"What do we need to do for you, guv?" asked Luke.

"Make ready for a fresh case," said Gus. "Most of the groundwork's complete. We transferred the Freeman Files for the Malone case last Friday, so we should be set to dive straight in to whatever he's chosen for us."

Gus kept his Bourbon treat for later. Kassie Trotter might have a sticky bun to offer him at London Road. Gus carried the black coffee to the lift and waved a silent cheerio to his team.

Every traffic light was in his favour on the return trip to Devizes. Even the red light at the roadworks on the other side of Seend obliged by turning green once he got within ten yards of the 'Wait Here' sign. Admittedly, it couldn't last.

As the Ford Focus puffed its way up Caen Hill, Gus remembered seeing the industrial-sized waste bins out in force as he drove through the town centre earlier. After a busy weekend's trading, they would overflow with waste and need emptying.

When your luck's in, the bin lorry is on the other side of the road. The stop-and-start dance began as soon as Gus crossed over the canal. Traffic leaving town was nose-to-tail, even at a few minutes to ten o'clock, and the workers struggled to position the big waste bins to discharge their contents.

After you've sat behind a large waste lorry watching the process once, you understand it. Gus watched and listened as hundreds of empty bottles cascaded into the giant maw at the truck's rear. Then he followed the vehicle another thirty yards for the process to begin again. This time it was mostly cardboard and other packaging materials in the bin. There was less noise, but the process was the same. Gus wondered why householders bothered to sort it.

After the third public house and the second fast-food takeaway, Gus sat in despair with his head on the steering wheel. The traffic lights changed ahead at the brewery, and Gus studied the lorry's indicators. Please don't turn left. Please don't. Yes, you beauty! The truck trundled over the mini-roundabout into the Market Square, and he could finally progress towards London Road.

Chapter Three

NOT FOR THE FIRST TIME. Gus found the last vacant parking space in front of the main Headquarters building on London Road. Making his way past Reception was never an issue these days. He met smiling faces rather than puzzled looks when he signed in at the desk.

Gus took the stairs two at a time. It seemed only fair to convince the ACC that he cared about arriving at the appointed hour. He knew overflowing waste bins wouldn't be a valid excuse any more than leaves on the line could explain the late arrival of the six-forty-five to Paddington.

"Late on parade again, Mr Freeman?" asked Kassie Trotter.

"I'm close enough," said Gus, "is he waiting for me?"

"Geoff Mercer hasn't finished his video conference yet," said Vera Butler, "so you're okay for a while."

"Good morning, Vera," said Gus, "did you have a good weekend?"

Kassie scowled at him.

The young girl hadn't entirely forgiven Gus for redefining the couple's relationship. Kassie had high hopes of buying a hat to wear at their wedding. Gus and Vera had enjoyed being together and had become more than friends. But sometimes, fate takes a hand. As far as Gus was concerned, the pair were happier as good friends.

"My weekend was hectic," said Vera, "but I understand you were busy too. My spies tell me you were in the Waggon & Horses on Friday night."

"Does that mean your spies weren't in the Fox & Hounds yesterday lunchtime?" asked Gus, "they're slipping. I was there too. Yes, the team wanted a night out on Friday to celebrate the successful conclusion of another case."

"We heard that Amelia went along," whispered Kassie, "she's a minx, isn't she?"

"So I've been told," said Gus. "Were you out on the town at the weekend, Kassie?"

Kassie looked forlorn. Her lovebird tattoos looked ready to drop off the perch. Gus wished he'd kept his mouth shut.

"Another Netflix box-set marathon, Mr Freeman," sighed Kassie.

The ACC's door opened. Kenneth Truelove beckoned Gus inside. As soon as he crossed the threshold, an out-of-breath Geoff Mercer hurried along the corridor from his office.

"Ah, Mercer, you decided to join us," said the Acting Chief Constable.

"Administration will be the death of me," said Geoff, "it seems our replacement Police Surgeon is taking time to obtain his release from South Wales Police."

Kenneth Truelove wasn't interested in the mundane vagaries of administration.

"Time to get the Crime Review Team started on another puzzle," he said, handing Gus the murder file.

"As you will see when you read this, Freeman, Grant Burnside was a much-feared criminal who twice walked free on murder charges. Someone gunned him down outside a warehouse unit that his family rented on the Cheney Manor Industrial Estate in Swindon. His eldest son, Gary, was inside the building with two employees. They had just arrived after driving from the Gorse Hill part of town. The killing occurred on the morning of Sunday, the twenty-fifth of May back in 2014."

"No rest for the wicked," said Gus, "they can't even take Sunday off."

"No doubt they were up to no good," said the Acting Chief Constable, "but there was a dead body to deal with first, and that took priority."

"So, whoever ran this investigation didn't check whether what they were doing inside related to what happened outside."

Geoff Mercer couldn't resist a slight smile.

"That's not what I'm saying at all," said the ACC. "Look, you need to read the file before passing judgment on how Gablecross handled the investigation."

"What was behind the killing?" asked Gus.

"Detectives believed it was a gangland execution. Burnside, sixty-five when he died, had built his criminal enterprise on drug deals and robbery. He died from a single shot to the head fired by a lone gunman. Gablecross officers heard rumours via confidential informants that Burnside was the target of a ten thousand pounds contract. That amount would have attracted several killers who operate in the county. Still, despite many hours of enquiries, they could not discover who ordered the shooting, let alone who carried it out. They identified two potential suspects for issuing the contract, Grenville Edwards and Manny

Franchetti. Those two men headed gangs in Bristol and Reading, respectively."

"One of those two wanted Swindon on their portfolio," said Gus. "So, initial thoughts were that it was the opening shot in a drugs war. No pun intended."

"Both gang leaders had solid alibis for the time in question," said Kenneth Truelove, "but that doesn't mean one of them didn't sanction the hit. Detectives found no evidence suggesting a known contract killer received payment from either suspect."

"Not that you would expect to find a trail of breadcrumbs leading to the killer's door," said Geoff Mercer.

"Police and paramedics arrived at the Industrial Estate at eleven thirty-eight," continued the ACC. "Burnside was in the driver's seat of the gang's Mercedes van. Four other men stood beside the van, waiting for the authorities to arrive. The paramedics had a wasted trip. The bullet drilled through the van's front window had obliterated half of Burnside's skull. Death was instantaneous. Officers found vomit on the floor by the passenger door. Gary Burnside confirmed that he threw up as soon as he opened the door to jump into the cab. Gary told officers they had arrived only minutes earlier, and he was opening the roller door to allow his men to carry out work inside when he heard a bang."

"Did they ask what work was so urgent it needed tackling on a Sunday morning?" asked Gus.

"They didn't get the chance," said the ACC.

That made Gus sit up.

"What do you mean?"

"I told you *four* men were waiting for the emergency crews to arrive. Gary Burnside, two of the family's employees and Patrick Iverson, the family solicitor."

"How did he get there so fast?" asked Gus.

"Iverson said that he received a call seconds after Burnside rang 999 and just happened to be motoring on the A419 towards Cricklade."

"That raises interesting possibilities," said Gus, "we might enjoy taking a closer look at this case."

"Iverson's a tricky customer," said Geoff Mercer. "He would have warned officers that they shouldn't press his clients to answer questions due to their traumatic experience."

"When did you read this report, Mercer?" asked the ACC.

"I didn't, sir," replied Geoff.

"Well, that's almost word-for-word from the senior officer's notebook concerning the conversation. Whether there was something untoward to discover, we'll never know. A significant time elapsed before anyone from Gablecross revisited the Industrial Estate. They had found no cause to search the premises, and when they returned, they discovered that young Burnside no longer rented the unit. He told the site owner that the area at the front of the building would always bear the image of his dead father's brains splattered over the back of the van's cab."

"What were they carrying in the van?" asked Gus. "If the Burnside gang majored in drugs and robbery, surely the van had to contain something incriminating?"

"Iverson allowed police to open the back of the van," said the ACC, "but it was empty. The senior officer noted that there was a slight whiff of cleaning products. However, Iverson argued that a business that kept its vehicles clean, taxed and insured shouldn't automatically attract suspicion."

"If they weren't delivering, then perhaps they were

collecting," said Gus. "Was there no CCTV on these premises back in 2014?"

"You'll need to check the murder file," said the ACC, "I can't recall the precise details."

"From what Geoff says about Patrick Iverson, they didn't make much headway on Sunday morning. Did forensics find anything useful when they got there to do their bit?"

"Not a thing," said Kenneth Truelove, "it's in the file. Detectives also conducted door-to-door enquiries in the vicinity of the Industrial Estate, but nobody heard or saw a thing. Of the occupied units on the Estate, only a car repairer was open near the entrance. Andy Wilkinson was working overtime that day and told detectives he was on his back under a Saab for most of the morning, with his radio tuned to Heart FM. A bomb could have gone off at the back of the site where the Burnside's unit was, and he wouldn't have heard it."

"That isn't very helpful, is it?" moaned Gus.

"What do you expect," laughed Geoff, "if it were easy, Gablecross would have solved it four years ago."

"What time did Wilkinson arrive? Did he see or hear the Burnside's truck turn up? When did the solicitor arrive? Why did young Burnside think they might need his help? We need to find answers to questions, and so far, I'm not hearing that those beggars from Gablecross ever pursued those lines of enquiry. What led to the rumours of the contract killing anyhow? Was there a turf war, or had Burnside's family done something more to offend them?"

"Each gang leader held a grudge against Grant Burnside," said the ACC. "A member of Grenville Edwards's family in St Pauls, in Bristol, got beaten up and hospitalised by two of Gary Burnside's colleagues. Denver Drewett and

Vic Hodge were allegedly the attackers, and those names appeared again in the report of the events on the Industrial Estate when Grant died."

"Surprise, surprise," said Gus. "If those two were enforcers for Burnside, that should have raised the alarm. Instead, the detectives swallowed the claim that they'd just arrived to carry out unspecified tasks. You couldn't make it up."

"Edwards had a solid alibi for the Sunday morning," said the ACC.

Gus was unimpressed.

"Apart from family members recuperating from a severe injury, how many other people does Edwards have on his books? Perhaps one of them drove up from St Pauls and shot Burnside. They should have checked a darn sight more alibis."

"There might be a 'why', Freeman," said the ACC, "but the 'why then' stumped the investigation team. How long would a lone sniper wait on the roof of a building on the off-chance Grant Burnside appeared? Whoever drove to Cheney Manor that Sunday morning knew Grant would be there."

"Why did the team waste time thinking it was a contract killing then?" asked Gus, shaking his head. "Just to square the circle, what did this Franchetti character have against Burnside?"

"Oh, that feud went way back," said Kenneth Truelove. "Grant slashed Franchetti in the showers while they were both in Winchester jail in the late-Nineties. Nobody saw a thing, of course, but the crudely fashioned blade opened Manny's cheek from under his left ear to his top lip."

"So, Franchetti waited for over fifteen years and then paid someone to shoot Burnside from a distance. Mmm, that does not make sense. It's too clean. With such a personal injury, Manny would want Burnside to know he was responsible for his death. He'd either use a blade on him face-to-face or stand and watch as one of his crew hacked him to bits with a machete. No, we need to dig deeper. There has to be another explanation. The killer knew where Grant Burnside was going that morning. Who knew? That's the first thing I want my Crime Review Team to find out."

"Good luck finding many people prepared to speak out," said Geoff Mercer. "The Burnside family are still the dominant force in Swindon. Gary assumed control after his father's death. There's an atmosphere of fear and intimidation in every quarter of the town, and the housing estates are rife with drug dealing and violence. In the past four years, the picture has changed for the worse. Drugs, knives, and guns are everywhere."

"So far, all I'm hearing is how solid this family unit is," said Gus. "Criminals don't publicise their activities for obvious reasons, which limits the number of people who knew Grant Burnside's movements. Was everything as tight-knit as it seemed? Why didn't anyone suspect that it might have been an inside job? A power struggle between father and son? What of the other siblings? You mentioned that Grant was sixty-five when he died, Sir. Did he have any brothers or sisters anxious to see a change of face at the helm of the enterprise?"

"Grant was the youngest of five children," replied the ACC. "George Burnside started the ball rolling as far as the clan's violent reputation was concerned. Crime was simpler back in his day. He tried to make a living by thieving, and if someone wouldn't hand over the goods, he wasn't shy about taking them by force. George used his fists in local pubs too, and on Nessie, his wife, at home. He brought his sons up to follow in his footsteps. I don't think drugs ever interested him. George was a racist and blamed the immigrants for bringing 'that muck' over with them."

"He didn't dissuade his sons from making their living from dealing the stuff," said Gus.

"No, but the older family members never followed that route," said the ACC. "It was Grant that thought it was easy money. Anyway, two of Grant's older brothers were dead by 2014, and the other one, Glyn, seventy at that time, suffers from dementia. After leaving prison ten years earlier, Glyn was never the same, and he faded into the background. Glyn's still around, but he's in a home and barely able to recognise his sister-in-law, Maggie when she visits by all accounts."

"I might take a closer look at Maggie," said Gus. "If Grant was handy with his fists like his father, then Maggie could have had the motive to have her husband killed."

"Stranger things have happened," said Geoff Mercer, "although I doubt that Maggie Burnside had access to ten grand without Grant or Gary knowing about it. Blokes like Grant Burnside keep their wives on a short leash."

"Are you sure you're allowed to say that?" asked Gus.

Geoff Mercer looked uncomfortable but realised Gus had his tongue firmly in his cheek.

"I understood what you meant, Geoff, and I agree. I check every throwaway comment for phrases that might trip me up with the PC brigade—times change. My late father referred to my mother as 'the ball and chain', and nobody batted an eyelid. Dad would never have raised a hand to her. He worshipped the ground Mum walked on. I'll get Luke Sherman to check whether Maggie Burnside had a bank or building society account in her name. Or whether everything went through a joint bank account with Gus needing to sanction every transaction."

"The other surviving child born to George and Nessie is Gina Burnside, born three years after Grant. Gina left home at sixteen and has spent most of her life as a prostitute. Gina was a regular in the Manchester Road and Broadgreen locality. After she left home, she never associated with the family again."

"Not the tight-knit family they would have us believe then, perhaps?" said Gus.

"I accept that Maggie could have had motive, Gus," said Geoff, "but I don't see Glyn or Gina being in the frame. Investigate Gary and his brothers, by all means."

"Gary assumed control after Grant's death," said Gus, "that was the term you used, Sir. Was he the eldest? Who decided who took control? Gary could have wanted to hurry the process along."

"Henry and Joseph are younger than Grant," said Kenneth Truelove. "Yes, Gary is the eldest child. There's a sister too, and she's the youngest at thirty-six. Her name is Kerry."

"Well, all four need closer scrutiny," Gus said. "Were there any follow-up investigations between 2014 and now? Or was that the only time Grant's murder came under the microscope?"

"You'll see a reference to a gang member called Howard Todd in the file. His sister reported him missing a week after Grant Burnside's death. Todd worked for the Burnside gang but never got arrested. The guys at Gablecross were sure that Todd reported to Henry Burnside, which marks him out as a dealer."

"Todd's not on the scene now, I take it?" said Gus.

"No sign of him dead or alive," said the ACC.

"I'll remember to get someone to talk to the sister," said Gus, "and we'll make a point of asking the Burnside gang what happened to him. Anything else?"

"Last year, Gablecross received a complaint from the neighbour of a retired pig farmer out Blunsdon way. A lady called Sylvia Kerr reckoned the farmer, Fergus McHugh, lit bonfires on the edge of her property at odd times of the day and night. The smoke drifted through the trees and caused havoc with the washing on her rotary dryer. Mrs Kerr accused McHugh of using accelerants because she saw flames high in the sky late at night. She feared he might start a forest fire during a dry summer. Uniforms went out to look. McHugh retired from farming in 2014 after he reached seventy-five, and the place is in a sorry state. The area where he lit the bonfires was a good half-mile from the farmhouse and surrounded by no more than a dozen trees. McHugh claimed he was getting rid of items he no longer needed now that he'd retired. When they returned to the farmhouse, McHugh said they might as well see the rest. The officers didn't know what he meant but followed him into a large shed in the yard. McHugh explained that he used to destroy dead pig carcases and other stuff in the steel container in the middle of the room. When asked what the bags stacked in the corner were for, he told them they contained caustic soda."

"Sodium Hydroxide," said Gus, "here we go again. That stuff is an ingredient in methamphetamine. Was McHugh admitting to brewing crystal meth?"

"Nothing sinister," said the ACC, "he was giving the officers the grand tour. If McHugh could sell the farm, he'd be off like a shot. Instead, it's fast becoming an eyesore. You can imagine that neighbours like the fragrant Mrs Kerr don't want their property prices damaged because they live next to a pigsty. I imagine the council will receive more and more complaints about the state of the place as time passes."

"Hang on," said Gus, "I must have missed something. Why were details of this complaint tagged onto the Grant Burnside murder file?"

"Fergus McHugh mentioned the name Burnside when the uniforms asked who he dealt with," said the ACC. "McHugh listed half a dozen people who sent him animal carcases for disposal. The officers recognised the names of local farmers. In Wiltshire, cattle and sheep rustling and the theft of valuable farm equipment soak up a significant amount of police resources. So, the officers came into regular contact with those farmers. Burnside's name didn't fit. When they queried it, McHugh reckoned they were mistaken. He hadn't meant Burnside. He must have mixed the name up with someone else. Gablecross probably thought it warranted taking a photocopy of the report and filing it, just in case."

"What could that mean, Gus?" asked Geoff Mercer.

"I don't know," said Gus. "Maybe this McHugh character's memory isn't what it was, and he genuinely mixed up a Burnside with something similar, say Heavyside. There's a farmer of that name with cows in a field right behind my bungalow. This case makes a change from the bare bones we started with on the Malone case. There are dozens of people to interview and loads of questions that need asking. I'm looking forward to hearing the answers."

"I suppose you want to head back to the Old Police Station to get cracking?" asked the ACC.

"Why? Do you have another item to discuss?" asked Gus.

"It's coffee time," said Kenneth Truelove, "and, as

Geoff mentioned earlier, we're working without a Police Surgeon for the time being."

"Well, you can't blame me for that, Sir. You fired Peter Morgan, and as I'm only allowed to work cold cases, I don't require his services. I rely on the autopsy reports in your murder files being accurate."

"Yes, hilarious, Freeman," said the ACC, "I was merely keeping you informed of our progress in getting the man we want. Rhys Evans works with the South Wales Police at their Headquarters on Cowbridge Road, Bridgend. He's single, thirty-two years old, and plays Rugby. Evans has the qualifications we seek."

"Why don't we use a general practitioner prepared to work part-time?" asked Gus.

"Other parts of the county *have* chosen that course of action. Our thinking is that since forensic physicians must be registered medical practitioners, then, ideally, they should have a higher qualification, such as a diploma in medical jurisprudence. Evans holds a DMJ, making him the perfect choice for the post here at Devizes."

"Are Bridgend digging in their heels?" asked Gus.

"They are, but they can only delay the inevitable," said Geoff. "I hope Rhys Evans will join us by the end of July."

"Why is it important that I hear this news?" asked Gus.

"Evans is single," said Kenneth Truelove, who had now stood and walked to the window to take up his favourite position.

The penny dropped.

"Ah, the prospective Police Surgeon needs a place to live. You immediately thought of my spare bedroom. Well, I'm sorry, but it's out of the question."

"What, you've already rented it to someone else?" asked the ACC.

"Not exactly," said Gus. "Why not ask Monty Jennings? Rental property is one of his successful enterprises. Not everything he touches is an abject failure. He buys up old properties, improves them, and rents them out. Vera lived in one of his cottages after they separated. Their divorce accelerated the need for Vera to buy a place of her own. Monty might have something standing vacant."

"I'll do that. Thanks for reminding me. At least we solved the Blessing Umeh accommodation problem over the weekend," said Geoff Mercer. "John Ferris phoned me last night to say they are happy to have Blessing stay at the farm."

"That came as a surprise," said the ACC, "I hadn't realised they had enough space."

"I don't see why it should surprise you, Sir," said Gus, "John and Jackie Ferris coped with three growing kids there for years. Suzie's the only one still there, but the boys' bedrooms are empty."

Gus spotted a glance pass between Geoff and the ACC. Was this a wind-up? If only he'd arrived earlier, he might have learned which rumours had reached London Road.

"Give that staff of mine a nudge, will you, Mercer," said Kenneth Truelove. "A chap could die of thirst in this place."

Geoff made to stand up, but there was a knock at the door.

"Methinks that someone was listening at the keyhole," said Gus.

The door opened, and in strutted Kassie Trotter with her trolley.

"Sorry, I'm lagging behind this morning," she said, "Vera has gone home with a migraine."

Gus kept his head bowed, pretending he was reading

the murder file. Kassie probably blamed him for Vera's condition too. Any chance of a tasty bun was receding fast.

"Blueberry muffins today, Mr Truelove. Can I tempt you?"

"Not for me, Kassie. I'll never get into my dress uniform if I succumb."

"I can do you a slice of Madeira this afternoon," said Kassie, undeterred. "It's light as a feather, unlike the girl that made it."

"Only one muffin for me today, Kassie," said Geoff, "Christine has spoken."

"What about you, Mr Freeman?"

"I'd love one, Kassie. Thank you."

"You're not under petticoat government yet, then?" Kassie asked as she presented Gus with his coffee and muffin.

"What does the grapevine say?" whispered Gus.

Kassie bent lower to whisper in his ear.

"Nothing new concerning you and Suzie Ferris, but Amelia Cranston had a big smile on her face on Saturday morning when I bumped into her in Morrison's. At least someone gets some action."

"Don't jump to conclusions without concrete evidence, young lady," said Gus, fearing the worst but still hoping for the best.

"No matter how long this dry spell lasts, Mr Freeman," sighed Kassie. "I won't resort to grabbing a married man to end it."

"I'm glad to hear that, Kassie," said Gus.

The young girl returned to her trolley and made a dignified exit.

"I worry about that girl," said the ACC.

"She's in a far better place than if you hadn't rescued her, Sir," said Geoff Mercer.

"How does that blueberry muffin taste?" asked the ACC.

"Scrumptious," said Geoff.

"Typical. If I was retired, I could put in a weekly order with Kassie and enjoy the benefits of her weekend baking without concern for my waistline. As it is, I'm stuck here for the foreseeable future."

"Has the PCC had a word already?" asked Geoff Mercer.

"Unofficially," sighed Truelove, "he called yesterday morning, just as my wife and I were leaving for church, to tell me I was the right person to steady the ship. I asked if they had advertised the position yet, and he told me he didn't envisage doing anything before next year. My wife has hardly spoken a word to me since."

"Not all bad news then, Sir," said Gus.

The ACC turned from the window and glared at Gus.

"That Focus of yours is making the car park look untidy, Freeman. I suggest you get back to work."

"Happy to oblige, Sir," said Gus. "The Burnside case promises to keep us busy."

Geoff Mercer escaped with Gus, and they left the ACC to finish his coffee in peace.

"Good hunting," Geoff said as Gus prepared to descend the stairs.

"I can't wait to read this murder file in full," said Gus. "Did you notice that the ACC never mentioned who ran the initial investigation? I'm betting someone who screwed up on an earlier case we've dealt with was running the show. It was Gablecross this and Gablecross that all morning."

"Theo Hickerton may have been on the team, but

'Colonel' Jack Sanders was still first choice DCI for a gang-land killing back in 2014. Grant Burnside's murder could have been one of the last high-profile cases he handled before he retired."

Gus jogged down the stairs to Reception, signed out, and went outside to his car. He didn't look up to see if the ACC was still watching.

Chapter Four

GUS MADE his way back to the Old Police Station office. He didn't complain about the frequent delays and the drivers ahead of him that didn't appear to know where they were going. He had too much on his mind,

This new case could be a tough nut to crack. And then there was DS Davis. He had already tackled the problems that DS Hardy and Lydia Logan Barre had presented. So it was okay for the ACC to drag him out of retirement and to team him up with a handful of youngsters. What the ACC hadn't warned him to watch out for were the hormones.

Alex and Lydia had become inseparable. Under normal circumstances, Gus should advise DS Mercer, and one of them would get re-assigned. But, because Lydia wasn't a serving officer, Gus convinced himself that as long as their work didn't suffer, it was something he could handle.

Alex's injuries from his motorcycle accident had caused him to become reliant on painkillers, and Gus had no choice but to suspend him until he recovered. Even then,

Gus had reasoned that Lydia wasn't to blame, nor did their relationship impact Alex's addiction.

If Kassie Trotter was right, and Neil and Amelia did more than meet up for a drink with the rest of the team last Friday night, then what should he do? Neil and Melody had just lost their first child because of a miscarriage. Melody was depressed and staying with her mother. Neil was home alone, and Amelia Cranston was a man-eater. Gus had seen her at close quarters while hunting for Terry Davis's killer and when Suzie disappeared.

There was no doubting Amelia's sharp-witted intelligence and ability to work under pressure. Geoff Mercer had suggested her as a prospective team member. If something happened on Friday night, then Neil Davis was an idiot.

After the threats Sandra Plunkett made towards the CRT's existence, Gus knew that if his team stepped out of line, they provided free ammunition to those who wanted the team disbanded.

Sandra Plunkett voiced the opinions gathered from several senior officers across the county force. Gus Freeman was a dinosaur, and the existing teams of detectives should handle cold cases. Every success that Gus and his team had only highlighted their deficiencies. The CRT wasn't popular in every squad room.

First, there was the problem of Alex and Lydia. Now, maybe Neil and Amelia were in a relationship, not to mention him and Suzie Ferris.

That situation wouldn't sit well with everyone, either. Well, Gus thought, as far as his relationship with Suzie was concerned, they could take a running jump. They were both single, and it was nobody's business but theirs. Perhaps he should have a quiet word with Neil, though?

Gus parked the Focus next to Neil's car and went up to the first-floor office. Three eager faces stared at him when he exited the lift. Gus looked around the office. The whiteboards were pristine and ready for action.

"Welcome back, guv," said Luke, "how was London Road?"

"Lined with trees and too much traffic, as usual," said Gus, waving the murder file. "I come bearing gifts."

"What have they landed us with this time, guv?" asked Neil.

"The shooting of Grant Burnside, a sixty-five-year-old gang leader from Swindon."

"Burnside? I remember my Dad mentioning that name," said Neil, "hard as nails. Not a bloke you wanted to upset. The entire family has been at it for years. Dad said Burnside's shooting was inevitable because he pissed off too many people, but they never found out who did it. Why do they believe we'll be any more successful, guv?"

"Because Gus is looking into it with fresh eyes," said Lydia, "and we find things the others missed."

Gus smiled.

"That's kind of you to say, Lydia, but there's a limit to the miracles we can achieve. This murder file has been lying around for four years, with no one thinking it warranted a second look. We've landed two other cases with several reviews, reconstructions, and TV appeals before they came to us. It makes me wonder why."

"Can you give us the basics, guv?" asked Luke.

Gus ran through the morning of Sunday, the twenty-fifth of May, four years earlier. Both Neil and Luke raised questions concerning the other family members' whereabouts. Gus answered where he could. However, those answers would remain hidden until they scrutinised the detail inside the folder.

"Any first thoughts?" asked Gus when he finished.

"The lack of CCTV out at Cheney Manor Industrial Estate shouldn't have been a big surprise, guv," said Neil. "It's obvious that Burnside rented a unit at the back of the yard because of the lack of camera coverage in the corners. Whatever they used it for would have been dodgy, and they didn't want an audience."

"I agree with Neil, guv," said Luke. "They needed a similar unit on another site after they abandoned the one at Cheney Manor. I wonder where that is and what they have inside it?"

"You need to get past Patrick Iverson to learn that, Luke," said Gus, "and that wouldn't happen without a warrant."

"Is Iverson still the family brief then, guv?" asked Neil.

"I don't think they can afford to let him go," said Gus. "He must be closer to their criminal activities than your usual solicitor. Whether he knows where the bodies are, I can't say, but I reckon he had a good idea of what was going on in the hours before Grant Burnside's shooting."

"What's our first step, guv?" asked Lydia.

"We'll get the photos of the murder site up on the boards, plus details of the key family members. I've already started a list of non-family members who could explain who killed Grant Burnside and why. Neil, if you and Lydia separate the elements of the file we need on the boards, Luke can set up the digital version for the Freeman Files. We should be able to make calls to our interviewees within the hour."

"I've spotted a familiar name here, guv," said Neil.

"DI Theo Hickerton, I presume?" said Gus.

"Not yet, guv. DS Jake Latimer was one of the first officers on the scene. He arrived thirty minutes after the initial
uniforms responded to the 999 call."

"Get on the phone and arrange to drive to see him first
thing tomorrow, Neil," said Gus. "We may as well use the
relationship you two forged on the Laura Mallinder case to
our advantage."

The team spent the day loading whiteboards with crime
scene images, street maps of Swindon, and photos and
backgrounds of the Burnside family and their close
associates. Next, Luke set up the Freeman Files, and as Gus
released the names, began arranging interviews that should
occupy them for the rest of the week.

"Do you have a preference for who accompanies you,
guv?" asked Luke. "Will we stick to the running order of the
names you're passing me?"

"We may need to adjust team selection as we go along,
Luke, but I'd prefer Lydia with me when we speak to the
widow tomorrow. Neil can spend most of the day in Swindon. Once we've finished with Maggie Burnside, I'll come
back here. You and I can then take a trip to confront Gary
Burnside."

"Got it, guv," said Luke.

"Gablecross has got me booked in for first thing, guv,"
said Neil.

"We'll have a chat before you leave tonight Neil. Don't
speak to Jake Latimer direct for the time being,
understood?"

"Whatever you say, guv," said Neil.

Gus thumbed through the names of people he believed
could provide the answers to Grant Burnside's murder. His
first interview would be with Maggie Burnside, Grant's
widow. She was less than six months older than him, not

that they had much else in common. Lydia might encourage Maggie to relax and say more than she intended.

If the Burnside clan operated as he believed it did, Maggie wouldn't go short of money. They would take care of her until she died. Odd how the word matriarch holds little relevance in today's world. Respect for their elders was universal in European and Asian cultures. Here in the UK, it was primarily the travelling fraternity and criminals that embraced it.

Gus imagined Maggie to be a gentle entrée to the main course tomorrow. A face-to-face with Gary Burnside, the current head of the gang. Patrick Iverson would be poised, ready to leap where a question demanded a straight answer. He could hear Gary practising his 'no comment' response already. Gus had ways to combat those tactics. He liked to encourage people to talk about their favourite subjects. If you offered men like Burnside an opportunity to tell you how great they were, they found it difficult to resist. Perhaps the odd word or phrase would slip past Iverson, the censor, and Gus could learn something valuable.

Gus had left Glyn and Gina off the list for the time being. He fancied discovering how Henry and Joseph ticked. They took after their mother in looks. Did that influence how they responded to Gary as head of the family and the gang? Could they have worked together to remove Grant as a pre-cursor to wresting control from Gary?

As for Kerry, Gus thought Neil would work best as the lead interviewer. He might sit in but play a watching brief.

When Luke checked the availability of the enforcers, Drewett and Hodge, the latter was in HMP Bristol. Hodge went to prison for demanding money with menaces in 2016. Drewett should have been in the cell with him, but he escaped before the police raided his house. His current whereabouts were unknown, although his mother did receive a postcard from Nesebar on Bulgaria's Black Sea coast last summer.

Gus wondered whether they should bother approaching Grenville Edwards and Manny Franchetti. When Gary agreed to meet with him without hesitation, Gus realised that the Burnside gang were no closer to finding Grant's killer than they were. Edwards and Franchetti were still alive, so neither did the deed themselves or paid for it. Luke could run a check on known associates in Bristol and Reading to discover if anyone had disappeared in the past four years. They could leave the two gang leaders on the back burner for now.

Luke received four names to add to the list Gus had passed across. It was half past four and almost time to call it a day.

Gus had added the names of Fergus McHugh, the old farmer and his neighbour, Sylvia Kerr. They were unlikely to add little more than background information. The same went for the third name. Andy Wilkinson, the car repairer, was working on the morning Grant Burnside died. The last name was Amanda Todd, Howard's sister. Hang on. There was at least one name missing.

"What about Patrick Iverson, guv?" asked Luke.

"Do we need a separate interview with him, Luke?" asked Gus. "We'll see him half a dozen times with the other family members. If there's something we think he can add, we'll grill him before and after each session."

"That might annoy him, guv," said Luke.

"Exactly," said Gus, "he might let something slip that helps us make progress. Anyone else you think I've missed?"

"Gary's wife, Kirstin, guv," said Luke, "surely she offers another insight into the Burnside family dynamic."

"Something tells me Kirstin will be present when we chat with her mother-in-law," said Gus. "Iverson will be with Gary, going through what they'll say when we meet them later in the day. The scheduling of the interviews wasn't an accident. I think Gary will instruct Kirstin to be his eyes and ears in our meeting with Grant's widow. We believed that Maggie was on a short leash while Grant was alive; it's reasonable to assume that Kirstin doesn't get treated any better."

Lydia, Luke, and Neil continued to prepare for the following day's interviews. Gus ploughed through the back pages of the murder file, searching for additional scraps of information that might get him a toehold in this baffling case.

At five o'clock, Luke and Lydia made their way to the lift. Neil Davis approached Gus's desk.

"You wanted a word before I left, guv?"

"A word to the wise," said Gus, "and a few tips for tomorrow's trip to Gablecross.

Five minutes later, they went to the car park in the lift.

"Goodnight, guv," said Neil, "I'll see you late tomorrow afternoon or first thing on Wednesday."

"Are we good, Neil?" asked Gus.

"We're good, guv," said Neil, "it won't happen again."

Tuesday, 19 June 2018

AFTER A FORTY-FIVE-MINUTE DRIVE FROM HOME, Neil Davis arrived at Gablecross Police Station, negotiated Reception, and searched for the detective squad hidden in the rabbit warren.

Neil knew he would recognise DS Jake Latimer. They had met on the Laura Mallinder case at the end of April and spent a crazy weekend interviewing girls from massage parlours across three counties. He was keen to learn how Jake had fared since they had worked together.

Gus had given him a brief rundown of the tactics he wanted him to use before leaving work last night. Neil was to plead ignorance of the case. Second, to encourage Jake or anyone else he collared to divulge more than if they believed the CRT already had the facts at their fingertips.

Neil also knew that Gus would appreciate a catch-up on what happened to DI Theo Hickerton. The DI hadn't covered himself in glory when he handled the original Laura Mallinder murder investigation. Hickerton reckoned the girl had brought it on herself through her choice of profession. Why waste valuable time looking for her killer? Sometimes life has a way of paying you back for your misguided actions. When they interviewed Tekin, Laura's killer stabbed Theo Hickerton in the chest.

Neil had reckoned that Ian Hewson, Laura's ex-boyfriend, had done it. The chat with Tekin should have been straightforward enough. Neil expected the Turkish barber to confirm that Hewson had been in the parlour that evening. Nobody guessed how much Tekin had loved his beautiful Laura.

As soon as Theo Hickerton posed his first question, Tekin lashed out with a blade fashioned from half a pair of his hairdressing scissors. The same weapon he'd used to stab Laura in the back in a frenzied attack. Love can be a strange emotion. The chest wound didn't prove fatal, but the affair ended Hickerton's hopes of further advancement in his career.

Neil pushed through the door into the squad room. It

was a hive of inactivity. Well, it *was* early, Neil thought. There were many empty desks, but Neil spotted the back of a familiar head on the far side of the room by the window.

"I see you've snagged yourself a desk with a view since we were here last, Jake?"

"Neil Davis, as I live and breathe. What are you doing here?" asked Jake.

"I called yesterday afternoon to arrange to talk with anyone who worked on the Grant Burnside murder back in 2014. Didn't the message get through? Where is everyone? It's far quieter here than when Gus Freeman and I were here ten weeks ago."

"They called several guys in for a six o'clock raid on addresses across Swindon. They were after the usual suspects, the villains living in Park North, Rodbourne, and Pinehurst. Our detectives won't be back before lunchtime. Early reports suggest they found a shitload of stolen goods."

"Never a dull moment," said Neil.

"Talking of which, you've had a right old time of it, haven't you? I was sorry to hear about your Dad, Neil. He was Marmite in this station. They either hated Terry's guts or thought he was a good copper. I never met him, but he didn't deserve that."

"Thanks, Jake. I don't know whether the news has filtered through yet. But, we identified the guy that killed him."

"It doesn't take long for good news to reach us, even this far north," grinned Jake.

"I suppose not," said Neil. "After working on the case immediately after Dad's murder, Gus insisted I take a break. So, while the others got involved in making headlines, I was sorting out Dad's affairs and heard events second hand."

"I get you," said Jake. "When your female DI got

herself kidnapped, and our Chief Constable topped herself, well, you can imagine the rumours that circulated within these four walls."

"That was perfectly understandable. Several of us met up for a few beers on Friday night," said Neil, "celebrating yet another cold case getting completed. There was also an extra victory to chalk up for the Crime Review Team. A result that might not reach the public domain for a while."

"The victory you're referring to relates to those rumours I mentioned, I take it," said Jake. "If it's under wraps, it smells like someone did something nasty on your doorstep. Am I right?"

"ACC Culverhouse from Portishead will get charged with the murder of Ricky Gardiner. Culverhouse and Sandra Plunkett paid Gardiner to kill my Dad to hide a hit-and-run accident they failed to report. A young man died in 2011 when Culverhouse and Plunkett returned from a Bramshill reunion. The Chief Constable couldn't live with the shame of the truth coming out about that and her involvement in DI Ferris's kidnapping. Gardiner got paid for that job too. Culverhouse was a chancer, even when he was my Dad's boss. He deserves everything he gets."

"I can't abide dirty cops," said Jake, "it's hard enough in this job when everyone is pulling together. I don't know how you keep up with everything at Devizes these days, Neil. Something happens every week. You know who gets the blame for that, don't you?"

"Gus Freeman, I suppose?" said Neil with a smile. "He gets the job done. I'll give him that. Of course, there was no way Gus was sitting on his hands when Suzie Ferris disappeared. He's got the hots for her."

"Hang on, wasn't he seeing somebody else when you

were here last? Someone in her mid-fifties. That DI Ferris is only a few years older than me."

"Gus and Vera are still good friends, as I understand it, but Suzie Ferris made a move on Gus before those two got too involved. From how she behaved around Gus last Friday, I reckon it's serious. The late Chief Constable must have recognised that too because she and Culverhouse made Suzie Ferris the kidnapper's target, not Vera Jennings or Butler as she is now. As for your other comment, I don't think Gus deliberately looks for trouble. He's just one of those coppers whose instinct tells him when something isn't right, and he can't resist following up on a niggle he gets until he's rooted out the culprit. We're expanding the team from next week because he's good at what he does, and the Acting Chief Constable wants as many cold cases off the books as he can get while Gus is on this winning streak. There are plenty of unsolved crimes on the list. It never ends, does it, Jake?"

"No, it doesn't," agreed Jake, blowing out his cheeks. "Yet we're far from being a prolific crime county. Heaven knows how they cope in the big cities, mate. Where are my manners? Do you fancy a cuppa?"

"I thought you'd never ask," laughed Neil, "I had nothing before I left home."

"What, the lovely Melody didn't get up to cook your breakfast?"

"She's staying with her mother at the moment," said Neil.

"Oh no, don't tell me another copper's marriage has gone down the toilet?"

"Melody suffered a miscarriage brought on by the stress of my Dad's death. She's struggling to get over it. We both are."

"Heck, I'm sorry, Neil. I had no idea. Me and my big mouth."

"It's okay, Jake. Melody's depressed; that's understandable. Her mother and I are working on bringing her out of it, but it's proving a long job."

Jake brought two mugs of coffee back to the desk.

"There you go, Neil. Have that. It'll put hairs on your chest."

"Well, now you know what's been going on in my world. How's your love life?"

Jake grinned.

"Who's the unlucky girl?" asked Neil.

"You know her, mate. I'm not fluent yet, but my Lithuanian is coming along."

"Janina?"

"That wasn't her actual name," said Jake, "Lina works at Tesco Direct now. I went back to visit her, semi-professionally, the weekend after you and I interviewed her. My rugged good looks and boyish charm persuaded her to agree to a proper date. It's early days, but it might prove to be the best thing I ever did."

"You lucky dog," said Neil. "One more thing before you tell me what you know about Burnside. What's Theo Hickerton up to these days?"

"As soon as he returned from sick leave, they transferred him to Traffic," said Jake.

"Oh, dear, the elephant's graveyard. How did Hickerton take that?"

"He's not a happy bunny, anyway; back to the matter at hand. I never got your message, Neil, because Hickerton helped lead that murder investigation. It explains why nobody told me you were on your way."

"Were you on his team back then, too, Jake?" asked Neil.

"For my sins, yes. Have you not heard of the Burnside clan?"

Neil shook his head. Jake might add to the knowledge he'd gathered yesterday.

"Let me fill you in on his background," said Jake. "Grant Burnside came up the hard way on Park North, one of the most deprived estates in the town. His father was a criminal, and he was always drinking when George Burnside wasn't inside. Young Grant got home from school to find George drunk, asleep on the sofa. His mother, Nessie, would tend to her cuts and bruises in the kitchen. Not a brilliant start for a lad. Is it any wonder Grant soon got into trouble himself? The older detectives here when I joined Wiltshire Police used to tell me stories about Grant. When he got nicked as a juvenile, he told the court he came from a broken home. He was looking for sympathy, of course, and believe it or not. It worked once or twice. Nessie kept the family together despite everything. Grant had four brothers and a sister. There was never a time when they got taken into care. So, the only time the home was 'broken' was when George returned from prison, got drunk, and smashed up the place."

"Are the brothers still around?" asked Neil.

"Only Glyn Burnside, and he's seventy now. He doesn't cause us any trouble. Glyn had early-onset Alzheimer's. Legend has it that Glyn was a handful, too, when he was in his teens and twenties. He had more fights than Rocky Marciano, but unlike the Brockton Blockbuster, he lost a lot more than he won. I think you can guess Grant's sister's name?"

"Um, does it start with a G?" asked Neil.

"They weren't very imaginative in the Burnside clan. Gina's still working if you're interested. She must be in her mid-sixties now, but she still struts her stuff on Manchester Road."

"I'll pass, thanks," said Neil, "so back to Grant's story."

"Well-paid jobs for those without qualifications were scarce when Grant left school at sixteen. So he started stealing on a more serious level alongside his brothers. He'd already got nicked for shoplifting and what's now called anti-social behaviour. After getting nicked a couple of times and spending their early twenties in prison, the brothers went to mainland Europe. Security was nowhere near as tight in shops and supermarkets over there. The brothers scheduled the trips to coincide with mid-week football matches. When Border Security staff spotted a crowd of Leeds or Liverpool supporters heading their way, they couldn't get them through quickly enough. Grant, Glyn and the others reckoned the cost of a replica shirt every few weeks was well worth it."

"I'm assuming Grant was head of the gang by then," said Neil. "Who else was involved, and what were they into?"

"Let's start with the family," said Jake, leaning back and relaxing in his chair. "Gary is the oldest son. He's married to Kirstin, who's eight years younger. A stunner is our Kirstin, but not that bright. She married Gary for his money and stayed as far away from his line of work as possible. Kirstin is the only adult Burnside family member I've met with no criminal record. Gary and Kirstin have two kids. One of each at the moment, until they get to junior school, and the teachers try to persuade them to try one of the dozen options available in this modern world."

"I've had no doubts about my sexuality, Jake, have you?" asked Neil.

"Stupid question, mate," said Jake. "You've met Lina. Anyway, I don't want to know how Grant and Maggie managed it with his frequent spells behind bars, but Gary has three younger siblings. Stay seated, Neil. I don't want you falling over in shock. Henry was next off the production line. He's single, forty-six years old, two years younger than Gary, and he controls the drug dealers. Grant and Maggie must have gone through the telephone directory to check which letters came next because Henry was followed by Joseph two years later. Joseph handles the traffickers and gets the goods to Henry. Another two-year gap followed, which might have been when Maggie decided enough was enough. They had a girl, at last, and she was named Kerry. When you meet Gary, you'll see that he takes after his father in looks. Six feet tall and sixteen stones of muscle. Henry and Joseph inherited a few of Maggie's qualities, which made them shorter and thinner."

"I take it nobody doubts that Grant Burnside was Kerry's father?" said Neil.

"Exactly, she's built like a brick outhouse and an ugly one at that. Funny how things even themselves out, though, isn't it? Kerry was behind the door when looks got handed out, but she's got more brains than the rest of them stacked together. Kerry controls the money side of the operation. Grant must have been proud that another female family member became an expert at washing and cleaning. That's what he thought women were any good for, apart from the usual. Kerry's money laundering skills are epic."

"Did someone tear pages out of the telephone directory Grant Burnside owned?" asked Neil. "Because they skipped a letter."

"Come on, Neil. There's no 'I' in team. Grant was thick, but even he worked out there wasn't an 'I' in gang either."

Neil groaned.

"Right, that's the family tree sorted out. Are there any important names on the lower branches?"

"Gary uses two old school friends for muscle," said Jake. "Denver Drewett and Vic Hodge. They've got the same pedigree. Both have been in trouble from nine and haven't learned that crime doesn't pay thirty years later. Vic's inside, and Denver's on his toes. We'll track him in time with the help of our European colleagues."

"This file doesn't look very thick, considering the number of faces you must have needed to interview," said Neil.

"One thing you need to remember, Neil," said Jake. "Whether it was DCI Sanders, who was gaffer back then, or DI Hickerton asking the questions whenever they sat opposite a member of the Burnside family, Patrick Iverson was always present."

"Patrick Iverson, who was he, their brief?" asked Neil.

"He's pushing seventy now, but Iverson's been the family solicitor for fifty years. Over that time, he developed a set of standard responses for the family to use."

"No comment?" asked Neil.

"That term gets used often," agreed Jake. "Iverson has a sense of humour, though, and he was pleased to sit and listen to Grant, Gary, or one of the other brothers use another two-word term."

"The second word being 'off', I imagine?"

"Exactly," said Jake. "As for victims who suffered at the hands of the Burnsides, or innocent bystanders who might have been potential witnesses, all we got from them was a wall of silence. Nobody dares to speak out against them. A couple have tried, and they disappear, never to be seen again."

"Have you got names?" asked Neil. "Perhaps Gus will want to interview their relatives. Time changes people's attitudes. Grant died in 2014. Someone might be ready to give us details of people who wanted him dead."

"I can give you two names of people who wanted Grant out of the picture," said Jake. "Grant made enemies as he clawed his way up from the gutter. He was the top dog here in Swindon, and nobody who opposed his meteoric rise survived. However, a gang headed by Grenville Edwards based in St Pauls in Bristol and another led by Manny Franchetti centred on Trafford Street in Reading wasn't best pleased when Grant shut them out of Swindon. We're talking of the days before county lines, and several outfits supplied various enclaves on the bigger housing estates. Grant Burnside put a stop to that. Regarding the brutal methods used by the gang as they took control, we interviewed people in their hospital beds after Grant's people attacked them. The same phrase cropped up repeatedly. It's my way or the highway. I told you, Grant wasn't very imaginative. He might have had a limited vocabulary, but it worked. Grant would never settle for a slice of the pie. He wanted the lot, so he took it."

Neil noted the names.

"Grant's been dead four years. Are Edwards and Franchetti still active?"

"Definitely," said Jake, "they were youngsters back then. Both Grenville and Manny are ten years younger than Gary."

"You mentioned people that disappeared," said Neil. "What can you tell me about them?"

"The closest example to the day Grant died was a dealer called Howard Todd. He was a chancer. My bet is he skimmed a percentage off the top, and Burnside found out."

"How did Grant handle people that crossed him?" asked Neil.

"We've never been able to find any of them to ask, Neil," said Jake Latimer.

Chapter Five

WHEN DS NEIL DAVIS signed in at Reception at Gablecross, Gus Freeman and Lydia Logan Barre left the Old Police Station to head for their interview with Maggie Burnside.

"Do you want me to drive, guv?" asked Lydia.

"Better not take your car," said Gus, "my old Focus won't attract any admirers. I'd hate to come out of Maggie's place to find your lovely Mini on bricks."

"Is Gorse Hill a dangerous place to visit then, guv?"

"Dangerous is too strong a word, Lydia," said Gus, "let's say several of the poorest areas in the town are within a stone's throw of where the Burnside family lived. Life expectancy can be ten years lower on the estates we're visiting than in neighbouring districts. Maggie Burnside is sixty-three; remember that when we meet her."

Gus drove through Royal Wootton Bassett to Gorse Hill. There was no rush. The forty-five-minute drive gave him time to think, and he parked outside Maggie's house at five to ten. Five minutes before the appointed time.

"Only one car on the drive, guv," said Lydia, "do you reckon that's Maggie's?"

Gus shook his head. He'd checked to see whether Maggie had a driving licence. It hadn't come as a shock to learn that she didn't. The Kia Rio GT that stood on Maggie's drive wasn't something Patrick Iverson would favour. Gus reckoned he guessed right. Kirstin Burnside was indoors, waiting for them to arrive.

Gus stood on the doorstep and rang the bell. Lydia lagged a few feet behind her boss and watched for the net curtains to twitch at the neighbouring houses. Lydia wasn't disappointed.

"You had better come in," said the attractive woman who answered the door.

Kirstin matched the description they had in the murder file. Thirty-nine and beautiful. Any money that husband Gary permitted his wife to spend went on smart clothes, shoes, make-up, and jewellery. Her ash-blonde hair, fake-tanned body, and immaculate nails suggested that Kirstin did everything she could to keep herself looking good for her husband.

Kirstin ushered the pair into the front room of the house. Gus imagined that Maggie spent most of her day in the kitchen-diner he spotted at the end of the hallway. The focus of this small room was the wide-screen TV suspended on the outside wall.

Maggie Burnside sat hunched over in a chair by the window. Lydia understood what Gus meant now. The tiny, wizened figure with a cigarette dangling from her lips looked at least ten years older than Gus. The ashtray on the arm of the chair was overflowing—the room stank of cigarette smoke.

"Mrs Burnside," said Gus, "we're from Wiltshire Police.

My name is Freeman, and I'm a consultant working with a Crime Review Team at Devizes. My colleague here is Ms Logan Barre. We're taking another look into the death of your husband, Grant. Four years have passed, and I'm sure the family still finds it hard. However, we will do everything to discover who shot your husband and bring them before the courts."

"Why now?" asked Maggie Burnside. Her voice sounded weak and husky. She stubbed out the cigarette and lit another. Lydia noticed that Maggie's eyes never moved from her while Gus spoke.

"We always do our utmost to find the killer in any murder case," said Gus, "but sometimes resources need to switch elsewhere before we are successful. That's where my team comes in. We can review the details of a case that's gone cold, jog a few memories, and prick a conscience here and there. We don't have another case to consider until we've exhausted every avenue or solved this one. Do you know what throws up more new clues than anything else?"

"How would I know?" shrugged Maggie.

"Asking questions that didn't get asked at the time. Sometimes, I ask relatives of the deceased, like yourself, if there was something the detectives didn't ask that you were eager to tell them. But they didn't seem interested, so you kept quiet."

"Maggie was at home that morning," said Kirstin, "there's no point trying to trick her into remembering something that didn't happen. She was asleep when Grant got out of bed. I spoke to her when I called her late morning. The next time I saw her was to tell her Grant was dead. Maggie never left the house."

"You called to tell her to get ready? That's the correct

term, I believe," said Gus, "Grant had decided to go out for lunch. Was that something you did often?"

Maggie shook her head and took a long drag on her cigarette.

"Once in a blue moon."

"Were you looking forward to it?" asked Lydia.

"Oh, you speak English then," said Maggie. "I wondered what use you were to the police unless you were interviewing foreigners."

"Well, Mrs Burnside," said Gus, "that's an unpleasant attitude you have. I'm surprised you haven't become accustomed to different faces and languages in Swindon, having lived here all your life. At the last count, there were around forty nationalities in the town. Time to accept it as normal, I should think."

"Whatever. I might accept it. It doesn't mean I have to like it," said Maggie. "I didn't mind going out to eat that day. It saved me cooking,"

"Where did you and Grant first meet?" asked Gus, changing tack.

"Just up the road in the park," replied Maggie. "A gang of us estate kids played together from when I was old enough to be outside on my own."

"How old were you when you went out with him?"

"Fourteen," said Maggie.

"Grant was twenty, is that right?" asked Lydia.

"Easy to work it out, wasn't it?" said Maggie, "Gary's forty-eight. I got pregnant at fifteen, never finished school, and we married when I was sixteen. I was expecting Henry when we went to the registry office. Grant never had any photos done."

"Would you say it was a happy marriage?" asked Lydia.

"Considering the times you had to cope with raising the children alone when Grant was in prison."

"You don't have a clue, do you?" sneered Maggie Burnside, "whether he was in prison or at home, it made no difference."

"It's alright, Maggie," said Kirstin, stroking her mother-in-law's arm, "don't let them get to you."

"Grant was a violent man," said Gus, "isn't that true, Mrs Burnside?"

"Grant kept me in my place. I knew better than to speak out of turn. He took after George, his father. People did as he said, or they felt the weight of his hand."

"That must have made you wish things were different," said Lydia. "Did you ever think how much better your life might be if Grant was no longer in it?"

"Walk out on him with the kids, do you mean?"

"Not necessarily," said Lydia.

"I never had him killed," screamed Maggie, getting up from her chair.

"Don't, Maggie. She's not worth it," said Kirstin, grabbing Maggie's arm and sitting her back in the chair.

Kirstin turned on Gus Freeman.

"You can't come here accusing people like that. You said you were going to solve Grant's murder. Gary's tried. I don't think he hasn't. He's tried to find out who did it every day for the past four years and got nowhere."

"So, despite Gary's best efforts, he couldn't discover who had Grant killed. Who did the detectives think was responsible in 2014 when they investigated his case for the first time?"

"People living in Reading and Bristol, men jealous of how Grant's business was growing," said Kirstin.

Gus smiled.

"Look, we're adults here, Kirstin. Everyone in this room knows that Grant was a convicted criminal. He made a living from thieving and drug-dealing. His father, George, was a thief and a thug. Your husband, Gary, has been in trouble with the law since his early teens. There had to be a list of people who wanted Grant dead as long as your arm. The police traced as many as they could in 2014, but nothing connected any of them to the shooting. Gary has taken the law into his own hands and examined several other possibilities in the past four years. Yet he still hasn't been able to put a name to his father's killer."

"We needed to press you on the possibility of it being an inside job, Maggie," said Lydia. "I didn't want to upset you, but we had to be sure you didn't play a part in it."

"I laid awake nights, wondering," said Maggie, lighting another cigarette. "Kirstin will tell you. These past four years have been the longest since I was fourteen without being covered in cuts and bruises."

Gus looked at Kirstin.

"Like father, like son?"

"We have our arguments. What couple doesn't? Gary's great with me and the kids. Whatever he gets up to when he's working, he doesn't bring it home."

"Let's go over that Sunday morning one last time, Maggie," said Gus, "why was Grant up so early?"

"He never said. He just moaned that he had to clear up a mess Gary should have sorted."

"I wonder what mess that was," said Gus.

"I knew better than to ask," said Maggie.

"Kirstin told us earlier that she called you late that morning to say your husbands wanted to take you to Sunday lunch. What were you doing that morning?"

"I hoovered downstairs and got the ironing up together.

I opened the windows to let in fresh air. Anything that would give Grant a fit if he'd been here."

"What were you up to, Kirstin?" asked Gus.

"Looking after the kids, bathing them, and playing in the garden."

"You didn't leave the house at any time to drive to the shops, perhaps?"

"No, Maggie and I did the shopping together on Saturday afternoon."

"What were you going to do with the children?" asked Lydia. "If the tragic news hadn't come through from Gary, would Grant have wanted your young children in the pub while you had lunch?"

"Not likely," said Kirstin, "I popped next door to my neighbour, Dawn, and she agreed to look after them for two hours. She still had them while I came here to comfort Maggie."

"Did Gary give any sign of how long he would be before he left home, Kirstin? What time was that?"

"A little after six. Gary never said why they were meeting. It was work. I knew better than to stick my nose in."

"You said 'they' were meeting," said Gus, "that would be Denver and Vic, wouldn't it?"

Kirstin nodded. She knew she'd made a schoolgirl error.

Gus was on a roll.

"So, Gary was meeting Denver and Vic, two enforcers who worked for the family business. Maggie reckons Grant's unusually early start was to sort out a mess that Gary should have been able to handle. It sounds dodgy, doesn't it?"

Gus glanced at both Kirstin and Maggie.

Blank faces stared back.

"No comment?" said Gus.

"Honest to God, we don't know what they were up to, Mr Freeman," said Kirstin, "and we didn't want to know."

"That's it for now, Mrs Burnside," said Gus, "I don't think we'll bother you again with questions. Rest assured, we'll get in touch if we discover who was responsible for Grant's murder."

Maggie Burnside didn't move from her chair. Gus and Lydia headed into the hallway with Kirstin.

"Thank you both for meeting with us today," said Gus. "We may have further questions for you, Kirstin. It rather depends on what we learn from our interview with your husband. No doubt you'll be in touch with him. Perhaps you'll jog his memory, and he can tell us what was behind that Sunday morning trip. Whether it relates to what happened later at Cheney Manor is anyone's guess. Good morning."

Kirstin closed the door behind them without a word.

"It's a pity I couldn't stay there for an hour, guv," said Lydia, "and encourage Kirstin to brew the three of us a coffee. You could have sprung that question on Gary, then. Now she'll warn him, and Iverson will have time to prepare a response."

"Who says I'm going to ask Gary what bit of business they had?" said Gus, "that question might be better aimed at Vic Hodge. He's in jail. Will Iverson be present, guiding his answers? Vic Hodge isn't the sharpest knife in the box. He might slip up or be prepared to give evidence as a quid pro quo. No, on the whole, I'm happy with the outcome. Let's get back to the Old Police Station and get ourselves a brew. That will give me time to think about how to uncover more hidden gems from Gary Burnside this afternoon."

"Thanks for having my back in there, guv," said Lydia. "I knew I was in trouble when Maggie gave me the stare while you went through your spiel in the first minute we were indoors."

"No problem, Lydia. What did you make of the place, anyway? If you could see across the room thanks to Maggie's chain-smoking."

"I know. I need a shower and a change of clothes," said Lydia. "Maggie's got a nice house, hasn't she? Crime does pay, after all. Family pictures everywhere and expensive ornaments. Her creature comforts surround her like a security blanket."

WHILE GUS and Lydia drove back through Royal Wootton Bassett, Neil Davis was thinking of lunch. He'd had a busy morning. After Jake had filled in the background of the Grant Burnside case, he'd wanted to pursue two further leads.

"How do I get in touch with this DCI Sanders?" he'd asked.

"Jack lives out at Haydon Wick, Neil, to the north of the town. It's pleasant enough up there, thousands of new houses, but a tad soulless. A perfect spot for a retiree. I'll chase up his address and phone number."

"Thanks. We'll get a better reception from Sanders than if we asked Theo Hickerton to speak with us."

"Ain't that the truth," said Jake. "The Colonel is happy to talk to anyone, Neil. Jack's a widower, lives alone, and enjoys gardening."

"Sanders sounds like a bloke that Gus Freeman enjoys visiting," said Neil.

"Anything more I can do to help you, Neil?" Jake had asked.

"Are you sure you can spare the time? Because I

remember how useful it was when you took us on a drive around the town to give us a feel for the place last time."

"You wouldn't mind a tour of the murder site, plus the estates where the Burnside family carries out their dirty business. Is that what you're saying?"

"Is that possible?"

Jake had looked at his watch, grinned, and grabbed a set of keys for a pool car.

"The Burnside family lived in Gorse Hill," said Jake as they drove through the busy streets. "Grant didn't move far from the house where George and Nessie raised him and the others. Gary's in a higher-class neighbourhood, as you would expect. Henry, Joseph, and Kerry are his neighbours. We won't do a drive-by because this car's a familiar sight on the streets. Burnside's people know most of our unmarked cars these days, and the word gets sent up the chain to warn them when we're on the prowl. On our left is the snooker club where Blake Dixon died back in 2013. That club has been the base for the Burnside gang for three decades."

"Who was Dixon?" asked Neil.

"Blake had been a regular on the nightclub scene since he arrived in town. I think he originated from Sheffield, but don't quote me. Blake had a string of customers across Old Town, and he became the primary source for party drugs in the eighteen months before the night he died. The Burnside gang had made their move. Grant was squeezing out the opposition, one by one. Either they rolled over and started working for him or got punished. My way or the highway. Blake Dixon wouldn't roll over, so they brought him back late at night. You would get no one to admit it, but there was one table still in use—a group of four lads playing snooker in the far corner of the room. Nobody knows what happened, but the Burnside heavies must have interrogated

Dixon, kicked him in the ribs and hit him in the head, based on the autopsy report. Then someone put the sawn-off against his chest and blasted him."

"What, those lads didn't come forward?" asked Neil.

"From what I heard, Grant sent the barman over with four bottles of Budweiser and said sorry for the noise, and the drinks were on the house. If anyone breathed a word, they would regret it."

"So, Blake Dixon disappeared the same as Howard Todd, I presume?" said Neil.

"His body never turned up," said Jake. "Heaven knows where they hide them."

"Do the Burnside family socialise together much?" asked Neil.

"Less now than in the days when Grant, Glyn and the older brothers were still around," said Jake. "They used that snooker club most from the late-Eighties through to 2010. Grant saw it as a quiet spot to mete out punishment for people who couldn't pay their drug debts. Gary and his brothers came to play snooker, drink, and then go to a nightclub. The attraction of snooker wore off, and in later years, they only called in when they had a problem to sort, such as Dixon. I don't know whether either of the younger brothers has been here since Grant's murder. Gary was the one who pushed the others into coming. He played pool in prison and won several snooker tournaments after he came out."

"Where do they carry out their punishment beatings now?" asked Neil.

"Search me," said Jake, "I wondered whether that warehouse unit in Cheney Manor might have been a favourite. It was remote enough that nobody heard their screams if the Burnside crew visited late at night."

"Or early on a Sunday morning," said Neil.

"No idea, mate. We never had time to look inside while they rented the place."

"Drugs are a menace whichever way you look at it, aren't they," said Neil.

"The picture keeps changing," said Jake, "and it never gets prettier. Cocaine has got dirt cheap, and it's so strong compared to what it used to be that people are having a cheap night out on it and drinking less. When Grant Burnside first got involved, it was an expensive commodity, and it attracted middle-class professionals and blokes in suits. The stuff is everywhere now, across every demographic, young to middle-aged."

"As long as Britain has drugs on its streets, then knife crime and street violence will continue to grow," said Neil. "Since the scourge of county lines gripped the country, it's fair to say that children are now on the front line in the war on drugs."

"I can't argue with that, Neil," said Jake, "kids between fifteen and seventeen are the biggest group involved in knife crime. Blokes like Henry Burnside target them to carry out violent attacks."

"Would you agree that the drug trade contributes to the mental health epidemic affecting young people in the UK?"

"Stands to reason, Neil," said Jake. "I know cocaine can cause paranoia, depression, and suicidal thoughts, but think of the problems those kids face from the intimidation and violence they witness every day. It wasn't like that when we were kids, thank goodness."

Jake turned the unmarked police car into the Cheney Manor Industrial Estate and headed towards the back of the lot. The unit looked nondescript. There was no signage to show who traded from the building.

"Are you sure the Burnsides' moved out?" asked Neil.

"Definitely," said Neil, "there's a firm of wholesalers renting this place now. They supply Indian restaurants across Wiltshire and Oxfordshire. Their vans will be out making deliveries now."

"It looks peaceful out here today," said Neil.

"Well, that was where Grant Burnside died," Jake pointed straight ahead. "The sniper was on the rooftop opposite. Directly above the unit where that reclamation firm is trading. A metal ladder's attached to the wall in the far corner on the left-hand side of the building."

"Not an easy climb," said Neil.

"You wouldn't catch me doing it, even with a harness," said Jake.

"If he reached there unseen, he could have arrived overnight," said Neil.

"He deserves a medal if he made that ascent in the bloody dark,"

"Forensics found nothing up there?"

"He was a professional. He didn't leave a thing. I read the report rather than climb up to check for myself."

"How did he get onto the site with no one seeing his vehicle? CCTV was active in some parts of the site, wasn't it?"

"He never appeared on CCTV, either in a vehicle or on foot. My guess is he came across the rough ground by the old pit. There's an angling club over there, but apart from that, it's never used much. A professional killer would get in and out without attracting attention. He didn't wander in the front gate for everyone to see, that's for sure."

"You still believe it was a contract killer?"

"I remember that was the initial thought," said Jake. "But we could never link the hit back to anyone on our radar. Nor could we find a connection to the many suspects for ordering the hit. But if it was random, would it have been so clean?"

"It's a puzzle, isn't it? Far more likely, a random hit would have been two shots from a handgun outside his house. Don't you ever wonder what it was all about?"

Jake turned the car around and headed for the exit.

"I need not tell you how many cases I've worked on since, Neil," said Jake. "If possible, when I finish working on a case, I file everything away for good. I don't lie awake at night thinking of burglaries that we never solved, or a rapist we caught but who never reached court, or who killed Cock Robin. That way is madness."

"I'll mention it to Gus Freeman when I see him," said Neil, "you might have got something there. Who wants to make a clean hit apart from a contract killer?"

"I'd better get back to Gablecross," said Jake, "the lads will be getting back from the aftermath of the early morning raids. You can drive back to base and put in your report. I hope you've got a better idea of how the land was lying back in 2014. We've moved on since then. Cocaine use has doubled, and violence is rife. The only thing that's stayed the same is that the Burnside family are right at the heart of it."

"How do they keep out of prison?"

"Iverson helps with that," said Jake, "plus the wall of silence they've established. Over the decades, they've manufactured an image of respectability with this so-called import-export business. We try to catch them at it, but they're one step ahead all the time. Take the county lines thing. We have people at the railway station watching for kids arriving from London. They know how many people are tied up there, plus the sniffer dog, and throw us the odd crumb. They sacrifice a pawn while the king gets protected at all costs. Meanwhile, they get the drugs onto the streets via another route. We can't be everywhere at once."

The two Detective Sergeants spent the rest of the ten-minute drive to Gablecross Police Station in quiet reflection. Jake parked the pool car and got out.

"I'll get going, Jake," said Neil, "my car is just there in the visitor's car park. Thanks for the background and the drive around the patch. It was great to catch up. Best of luck with Lina. I hope it continues to go well."

"Don't leave it so long next time, mate. I hope Melody gets better soon too, Neil. I've no idea whether we'll ever be thinking of starting a family, but I pray nothing so horrible happens if we do—anyway, good luck with the case. You've got your work cut out. Say hello to Gus Freeman for me, will you?"

With that, Jake disappeared inside the Gablecross labyrinth, and Neil crossed the car park to his car. He could return to the office within the hour if the traffic were light. He checked his watch. Gus and Luke would be interviewing Gary Burnside now. Neil hoped he could get away early tonight. He needed to sort out his personal life.

"WHAT WAS your thinking behind choosing this place for the interview, guv?" asked Luke.

"I wanted a place that felt like neutral territory for both parties," said Gus, "but was official enough to make Gary Burnside uncomfortable."

Gus and Luke sat outside Marlborough Police Station. Gus had called DI Trefor Davies to ask if an interview room could be available for an hour this afternoon. Trefor owed them a favour and was happy to oblige.

"Don't leave it in a mess," he said.

"We'll be on our best behaviour," Gus promised.

Once inside the building, they soon found Trefor, and he showed them into the room.

"I'll leave you to get yourselves set up," he said. "Your guests should arrive in five minutes. I'll get one of my civilian staff to bring them through. It might help lull this Burnside character into a false sense of security."

"With Patrick Iverson on hand, there's only a tiny chance of that, Trefor," said Gus, "but I live in hope."

Five minutes later, there was a knock on the door, and a middle-aged back-office clerk showed Iverson and Burnside into the room.

The solicitor was tall and thin, wearing a dark suit, a pale blue shirt, and a tie. It belonged to a solicitor's society whose members Gus had previously met.

Gary Burnside hadn't bothered to dress for the occasion. This meeting with the police only warranted a short-sleeved polo shirt and designer jeans. Gus corrected himself. Gary had gone to the trouble of adding bling. Three gold chains around his neck, plus the large gold watch on his right wrist.

"Good afternoon, gentlemen," said Gus, "please be seated. Thanks for coming this afternoon. This room was halfway between us and seemed to set the right mood. My name is Freeman, and I am a consultant with Wiltshire Police. DS Sherman works for me with a Crime Review Team. It's over four years since your father's murder, Gary, and we believe it's time to take another crack at finding his killer. Kirstin tells me you've had no joy using whatever sources you made available."

"Whatever methods Mr Burnside used, they were

perfectly legal," said Patrick Iverson, "I hope you're not insinuating otherwise?"

"It surprised us to find you here this afternoon, Mr Iverson," said Gus. "After all, this is an informal chat, in which we wanted to assure your client we were coming to this cold case review with an open mind. There's no use going over the same ground my colleagues covered back in 2014. This is a fresh start. I'm surprised you're trying to suggest that your client is squeaky clean. I have his criminal record here in front of me. It makes for interesting reading. At this stage, I'm not concerned with the tools and techniques Gary and his staff utilised while trying to discover who killed his father. That's not my concern. My job is to review the circumstances of the day of the murder, and by the end of this get-together, I wish to achieve three objectives."

"My client will co-operate in any way he can, Mr Freeman," said Iverson, "but if I feel the questioning strays from your narrow brief, then I will advise my client not to answer."

"Because he might incriminate himself, do you mean?" asked Luke.

"Certainly not," said Iverson, "on the grounds it might not be in his interest to answer."

"What three things do you want to know?" asked Gary Burnside.

"Your wife, Kirstin, told us this morning that you left home a few minutes after six on the day of the murder. What time did you arrive at Cheney Manor Industrial Estate?"

"Around twenty past eleven, give or take two minutes,"

"Denver Drewett and Vic Hodge were with you when you visited your warehouse. Your father drove the four of you to the site. You were inside the building, opening the roller doors when you heard the single gunshot."

"We didn't know it was a gunshot. We thought it was a car backfiring."

"Sorry, Gary, that wasn't a question. I'm merely piecing together the sequence of events after reading the murder file prepared by the detectives at Gablecross. There's no dispute that the sound was a gunshot. The crime scene photos confirm that your father died from a single shot from a sniper lying on the rooftop of an adjacent unit. I'm more interested in the time."

"It's simple enough, isn't it?" said Gary, "Dad drove into the Industrial Estate, parked outside our unit, and I unlocked the side door. Denver and Vic followed me inside, and I started to open the roller doors."

"When we spoke to your mother, Maggie, this morning, she confirmed that Grant left home after seven o'clock. She didn't know where he would go or who he would meet. So when Kirstin called at around a quarter past eleven, it was to tell Maggie about a hastily arranged family lunch. Maggie never expected Grant to arrive home at any particular time. She just knew she needed to be ready to jump, to do whatever her master required."

"Is this leading anywhere," asked Patrick Iverson, "I thought you wanted answers to three questions?"

"Forgive me if I appear to ramble, Mr Iverson. I retired four years ago now, and sometimes events as complicated as this only make sense when I step through them one at a time. I hope to hear an explanation of the confusing parts from those who were there, people like Gary. The words on the page in the murder file don't always give the full picture. Do you have anything to offer, Gary? To help me understand what life was like growing up with Grant Burnside, knowing what he did for a living, and how people feared him?"

"I listened to him reminiscing with his older brothers about things their father George used to do," said Gary. "When you're a Burnside, you know what it means to be poor and to fight your way to the top. Nobody gives you a chance. You have to take it."

"So, the lesson you learned at your father's knee," said Luke, "was that the only way to make it in this world was to steal from others. Did he explain the downside to the career path he set you on?"

Gus watched Patrick Iverson stiffen in his chair. He was wary of how this was going, but Gary Burnside looked more relaxed than he had been five minutes earlier.

Gus thought his tactics might have borne fruit. Gary couldn't resist telling them how good things were when you were a member of the Burnside family. Softly, softly, as another policeman used to say.

Chapter Six

GUS SAT BACK and let the story unfold.

"It's a ladder you must climb," said Gary Burnside, "according to my Dad. He started with shoplifting, then moved to small retail outlets. Places that they used to call shops when there were High Streets in every town. He reckoned it was five to ten years before he was proficient enough at his work to attempt a building society or a bank."

"The further you climb, the more likely you'll get caught. So you can expect to do serious time when you slip up, " Gus said.

"Dad always told us that if we got nicked, we should resign ourselves to it straight off and quit messing. He reckoned it wasn't difficult to survive inside when you're a hard man. The other prisoners leave you to get on with it, and you can learn new tricks while you're inside. Tricks of the trade that stand you in good stead when you get out. So he suggested that we spent hours in the gym, preparing for any jobs we might do when we got out."

"You must understand that this is hypothetical, Mr Freeman," said Iverson, "not an admission of guilt. My client merely recalls things his late father suggested they did to stay safe if they ever found themselves in prison."

"Yeah, that's what I meant," said Gary, "we run a legitimate import and export business these days."

"I recall you got nicked first when you were twenty-seven," said Luke. "I imagine you did your time standing on your head. What new tricks did you learn while inside?"

"I studied computers," said Gary, somehow keeping a straight face.

"What age are you now, Gary, forty-eight?" asked Luke. "when did you move up the ladder and get involved in drugs?"

"I've served my time," said Gary Burnside, "you can't connect me to any of that caper these days. Things have changed since Dad's generation. Youngsters today don't bother with that ladder anymore. Why tackle a security van when you can make more money dealing drugs? When I was in my thirties, firms on this side of the English Channel were the big noises in the European black market. Drugs were what mattered most. Nobody bothered sweating the small stuff. They sold pills and weed at school and then moved on to hard drugs in their teens. Nothing else matched the return on investment of time and money. It still doesn't, so I've heard. I'm best out of it."

"So, the gym work was for keeping fit while inside," asked Gus. "Not hardening you up for a life of crime, plus getting the groundwork done on how to put the frighteners on people when they didn't play ball."

"I think you've got me confused with someone else, Mr Freeman. That doesn't sound like anyone I recognise."

"If you study the company accounts, you would understand that you're barking up the wrong tree," said Patrick

Iverson. "If you produced the correct warrant, our chief financial officer would be happy to take you through them."

"Would that be the copy you provide to HMRC or the real ones?" asked Gus.

"If Gablecross had anything of substance, we wouldn't be attending this informal chat," said Iverson. "Can we return to your brief of discovering who killed my client's father?"

"Computers didn't have a thing to do with what you did that Sunday morning, though, did they, Gary," said Gus. "Not with your father and thugs liked Drewett and Hodge in tow. I suspect what occupied nearly six hours before the emergency services arrived involved another activity. You said that while inside, you spent time in the gym preparing for future work. I suggested you also perfected the art of intimidation and punishment for those who were unwise enough to fall behind with their payments or, worse still, cross you. Isn't that closer to the truth?"

"No comment," said Gary.

"I wondered how far we'd get before we heard that phrase. Well done, Gary," said Gus, "you didn't need a prompt from your solicitor. He's trained you well."

"This is a complete waste of time," said Gary.

"I'm glad you raised that matter, Gary. Mr Freeman mentioned earlier that the time interested him," said Luke. "What he's struggling with is why you needed to leave home so early if you weren't due at Cheney Manor until after eleven. We know you had to get to Drewett and Hodge's homes to collect them. I've checked the addresses, and it's a tidy distance for a walk. I doubt that would be high on your wish list. It doesn't give the right image. Perhaps you drove."

Silence reigned on the other side of the desk.

"Grant left his home in Gorse Hill at seven," said Gus,

"and we know that he drove the Mercedes truck onto the site at a little after eleven twenty. There was no mention of another vehicle. We guess that Gary drove the Mercedes to pick up his mates and then collected Grant. Where you drove next is a mystery. So is the reason behind the change of driver. One might assume that Gary spent time out of the truck, maybe with Denver and Vic, while Grant stayed with the Mercedes. After you were ready to move on, you returned to the truck, and Grant drove out to Cheney Manor."

"You have a vivid imagination, Freeman," said Patrick Iverson, "there are a hundred other explanations for what they did between six and eleven."

"Give us one supportable alternative," said Gus. "Show me where my interpretation of events went wrong."

"No comment," said Gary.

"If you have nothing to say, Gary, then I'll continue to theorise how things might have progressed," said Gus. "You told the police that Denver and Vic were there to carry out work for you. The truck was empty. So, whatever you did between seven and eleven didn't involve bringing anything to Cheney Manor. It must have been inside the unit already."

Gus spotted the furtive glance from Gary to Iverson, but the wily solicitor didn't react. His stony face didn't flinch.

"I don't believe the police checked what was behind those roller doors you were so keen to open," said Gus. He pretended to flick through the murder file to verify that statement.

"There was nothing to show that the contents of the warehouse unit in any way connected to Grant Burnside's murder," said Iverson. "I cannot see how you'll find his murderer by concentrating on that aspect of the morning's events. Instead, you should look for the gunman on the roof."

"Have you seen or spoken to Howard Todd recently?" asked Gus.

"Who?" asked Gary.

"Oh, come now, Gary. Howard was a dealer who reported to your brother, Henry. It's four years since he last worked for your family, but surely there haven't been many former employees that disappear without a trace?"

"Toddy must have moved on," said Gary, "why not ask Henry where he fitted into his side of the business? Todd was nothing to me."

"Now, that I can believe," said Gus.

"I'm struggling with the roller doors," said Luke.

"I reckon you're both struggling," said Gary, "when are you going to ask these questions you were banging on about?"

"DS Sherman means that if the Mercedes was empty, Grant didn't need to reverse the van up to the roller doors. You weren't there to deliver something. Therefore, there was something inside that needed their attention. We can only speculate, but one explanation for Grant reversing the van as he did was that after your men completed the task, the said item was to go in the back. The Mercedes was there for removals."

"No, you've got it wrong," said Gary, "Dad didn't need to reverse the Mercedes that time. The gunman wouldn't have had a shot if he'd only stopped facing the doors. He'd still be alive. There was no reason for Dad to get out of the cab. We were only going to be inside a few minutes."

Patrick Iverson tapped Gary on the arm.

"Could we take a break for a moment, please? I want a private word with my client."

"We need a moment longer, Mr Iverson," said Gus, "and then you can chat with your client all afternoon."

"When did you first arrive at Cheney Manor Industrial Estate that morning?" asked Luke.

"No comment."

Luke looked at Gus. Both men had answered in unison. It seemed likely that was the signal for Gary Burnside to refuse to answer any more questions today. Was Gus happy with what they'd learned? Gus nodded to Luke. That was it for now.

"Let's take a break," said Gus, "thanks for travelling here today, gentlemen. It's been most productive. I'm sure we'll have further questions, and we hope to continue with this informal setting for future meetings. If we uncover something that connects you to criminal activity, we'll pass it on to the detectives at Gablecross. They might proceed on a more formal basis. Arrests and cautions, that sort of thing. We can avoid such unpleasantness as long as we understand one another."

Iverson and Burnside left the room without a word.

"What do you reckon, guv?" asked Luke.

"When did you find out they had been there earlier?" Gus asked.

"I didn't know that they were," said Luke, "I was putting forward an alternative version of events. One of the hundred that Iverson mentioned. Is it fair to interpret that swift no comment as an admission that they had been there earlier? Have you been thinking along those lines already?"

"I didn't have enough facts to make a statement with any certainty," said Gus. "It crossed my mind, as did something else about the gunman. Gary could have meant that Grant reversed up earlier when there *was* something in the back of the van. With it halfway into the unit and the back doors open, Drewett and Hodge could have taken whatever they had inside into the unit with no one being the wiser. Grant simply made the same manoeuvre with the van when they returned out of habit. The sniper relied on that manoeuvre. He stayed on the roof overnight, lying in wait. Perhaps Grant was out of the van and inside the unit before he lined up the shot, so he waited for a better opportunity."

"I wonder where they drove to after they left the warehouse?" asked Luke.

"You're nearly there, Luke," said Gus.

"How did the gunman know that they were coming back?"

"You've missed a step. But let's follow your thoughts first. I think the timing of the phone call from Kirstin to Maggie is vital," said Gus. "Out of the blue, Grant and Gary want to take their wives for a Sunday lunch. Maggie said that didn't happen in a month of Sundays. The men had something to celebrate. Whatever they started at six was almost finished. The last thing they had to do was collect Drewett, Hodge, or both from the warehouse."

"You think someone stayed behind," said Luke, "and the gunman realised that the van must be returning. He just needed to be patient."

"Right, Luke," said Gus, "you've explained how that piece of the jigsaw could fit together. What about that missing step? It should be easier now you've worked out that someone stayed behind."

Luke thought for a minute and then smacked the desk.

"What happened inside the unit when all four men were still there? Why did Drewett and Hodge need to stay? Where did Grant and Gary Burnside go, and why?"

"Was the warehouse unit being used to store supplies of drugs?" said Gus.

"That's possible," said Luke, "but Joseph controlled the trafficking, and Henry controlled the dealers. Why would Grant bother with the day-to-day stuff his sons were supposed to handle? Did they need a large Mercedes truck to move a few kilos of cocaine? Drewett and Hodge were at the unit to work on something. They were enforcers, not dealers, traffickers, or tradespeople. Their role was to hurt people whenever ordered by one of the Burnside family."

"Maggie told us this morning that Grant moaned about getting up early to clear up a mess that Gary should have sorted."

"Gary was the eldest brother and number two in the organisation. So, that suggests that someone stepped out of line, and Gary hadn't dealt with it in a timely fashion."

"Which leads us to our friend, Howard Todd," said Gus.

"The dealer reported missing by his sister, Amanda, on Monday the second of June," said Luke.

"Todd's last sighting was on Saturday, the twenty-fourth of May, according to the murder file," said Gus. "CCTV caught him near Ainsworth Road."

"Gary got his two mates to help him find Todd hiding on his usual patch. Then Grant picked them up in the Mercedes and drove to Cheney Manor. It sounds as if Todd had a one-way ticket."

"When the truck left the site, they were off to dump the body," said Gus. "They left Drewett and Hodge to do a clean-up job. At twenty past eleven, Grant returned. Gary was with him because that was when he called Kirstin. She then rang her mother-in-law."

"It explains a lot," said Luke. "It explains why the back of the truck was so clean and why the uniformed officers smelled bleach as soon as they opened the doors. No wonder Iverson didn't want the police to look inside the unit."

"I might have been wrong about Fergus McHugh," said Gus. "He meant Burnside when he gave the police a list of his customers. He used that gadget in his shed to dispose of Howard Todd, boiled him for several hours and poured him down the drain. Tell Gablecross to tread with care when they speak with Todd's sister, Luke. There's no need to give the poor woman nightmares."

"How does any of this help us find who killed Grant Burnside, and why, guv?" asked Luke.

"You're no fun, Luke. Let's drive back to the office and catch up with whatever Neil's uncovered. I'm afraid you're right. We're no further forward on that score. First thing tomorrow, I suggest we get our heads together with the others to thrash out an alternative approach."

They found Lydia alone in the office when they returned to the Old Police Station and exited the lift. Gus glanced at the clock on the wall. Four thirty-five. Surely Neil wasn't still at Gablecross?

"No sign of Neil yet?" he asked.

"He's been and gone, guv," said Lydia. "Neil had something to sort out in Devizes. It sounds as if he had a busy day with DS Latimer. Neil's put everything he learned into the Freeman Files. So you can bring yourself up to speed. He'll be here bright and breezy at nine in the morning, ready to go to his next interview. Did you decide who was next on his list yet?"

"I had, but it might need a rethink. You and I uncovered scraps of knowledge from the female members of the Burnside family related to events on the day of the murder. Luke and I encouraged Gary Burnside to tell us how to piece those scraps together. The trouble is that it has left us with more questions than answers. So first thing tomorrow, I wanted to thrash out a different plan of action. Perhaps Luke and I should add our thoughts from this afternoon's interview to the files. Then I'll take a copy home tonight to understand the revised big picture."

"I'll get started on my part now, guv," said Luke, "I agree with you. There's little point in ploughing on with the interview schedule we have at present. So before I go home, I'll put in calls to postpone those I've arranged for tomorrow. Then, after you've reassessed the situation overnight, you can advise me on what to do with those booked in for Thursday and Friday. And we can prepare a revised list."

"Fair enough, Luke," said Gus, "I'll update the files with my stuff first while it's still fresh in my mind. Then, a read-through of Neil's impressions and recommendations must come next. There might be something there that is a game-changer. I sincerely hope so because we seem to be in reverse gear so far."

"Does anyone know why Neil was in a rush to get back to Devizes?" asked Luke.

"His head has been all over the place, Luke," said Lydia, "I'm not surprised that something cropped up that he'd forgotten. It could be a family birthday or anniversary that slipped his mind. Today was his busiest day since returning to work. Maybe it tired him out more than he thought."

Gus kept his thoughts to himself. If Neil had taken his advice to heart earlier, then PC Cranston should get let down gently a few minutes after five o'clock. Gus hadn't asked just how far things went on Friday night. He didn't want to know.

If Neil wanted to remain a member of the Crime Review Team, the married detective had no illusions that he had to quit cheating on Melody.

"I hope he gets a good night's sleep," said Gus, "because things could get busier than ever around here."

Gus opened the Burnside file on his computer and added notes for the interviews with Maggie, Kirstin, and Gary Burnside. As for Patrick Iverson, Gus merely included a brief comment for now. He was everything that the ACC and Geoff Mercer had warned him he was. The solicitor was slippery as a bag of eels.

As Gus collected his thoughts and stared at his computer screen, Lydia laid a hand on his shoulder.

"I'm off home, guv. I'll see you in the morning."

"No problem, Lydia. Enjoy your evening."

"I'm driving over to see Alex," she said, "he had a physio session this afternoon. He'll need a quiet night in front of the TV. I'm feeling my age at twenty-five. Heaven knows how Alex feels. He's over ten years older than me."

Gus had just finished typing his notes on Maggie Burnside. She was only six months older than him and looked like death had an icy hand on her shoulder. He didn't look that decrepit, did he?

Who do you ask about things such as that, anyway? Friends lie to you because they don't think you want to hear the truth, and only an idiot asks a stranger or an enemy. So maybe it was better not to know. Gus continued believing he looked good for his age.

Luke stayed until a quarter past five, and then he made for the lift.

"Nicky's picking me up, guv," he said as he passed Gus's desk, "we've got an hour of squash booked at the leisure centre for six o'clock. Nicky's a far better player than I am. Thirty minutes will shatter me, but every little helps us keep fit."

"See you in the morning," said Gus.

After the lift door closed, he groaned. Everybody was at it. Gus called it quits at six, collected a digital copy of the Freeman Files and drove through Devizes on his way home. He kept an eye open for Neil Davis and Amelia Cranston, but there was no sign of either of them. Fingers crossed that went smoothly, he thought.

Gus slowed as he drove past the gateway to the allotments. He thought about stopping to check whether Bert Penman had returned to his usual work pattern. He couldn't see anyone working there this evening from the road, and Clemency Bentham was elsewhere, tending to her flock of parishioners. Gus drove up the lane, pulled into the driveway of his bungalow, and parked the car.

There was no sign of his having company this evening so far. He and Suzie had made no firm arrangements after she left early on Monday morning to return to the farm in Worton. Although several casual clothing items now hung in his bedroom wardrobe, her uniform remained at home.

Gus went foraging in his fridge and freezer cabinets, searching for something to match his mood. Every other team member seemed to be on a health kick. Even the ACC and Geoff Mercer refused a blueberry muffin from Kassie Trotter this morning. So what did he have that was good for him?

After five minutes of hunting, he gave up. Gus cut two thick slices from a crusty, wholemeal loaf, covered them with real butter, and made a sandwich with the few scraps of salad ingredients he had available. Lettuce, spring onion, radish, tomato, cucumber, and beetroot looked healthy enough. A cold beer helped wash it down.

Gus uploaded the digital file to his computer and reviewed Neil's contribution. There was plenty of valuable background, but Jake had provided no new clues that might help discover who killed Grant Burnside. Nothing had changed since Jack Sanders, and Theo Hickerton had either given up on the case or got transferred onto something with a higher chance of success.

Jack Sanders sounded like a fascinating character. He'd been at Gablecross for years. Gus had heard glowing reports of the DCI while working on his own cases in Salisbury. Sanders was a straight arrow, making Gus wonder how he put up with Theo Hickerton as his second-in-command.

Before reviewing their approach to the Burnside murder, Gus reckoned it was worthwhile taking a trip to Swindon to chat with the retired DCI off the record. Gus called Sanders, and the pair agreed to meet at ten in the morning. Gus remembered Luke saying that he wouldn't be home yet, so Gus rang and left a message. Luke could keep Neil and Lydia occupied until he arrived in the office. Another half-day wouldn't make Grant Burnside any less dead, and they weren't getting anywhere with the information they had gathered to date.

As the evening passed, Gus wished he hadn't eaten so healthily. There were good reasons for never combining items such as onion and radish in any dish he prepared. As night fell and he drew the curtains in the lounge, he poured himself a glass of red wine.

It was unlikely to cure his wind, but he needed to spend an hour deep in thought before going to bed. He convinced himself it deserved a nightcap.

Wednesday, 20 June 2018

AT LEAST GUS hadn't drunk too many glasses of red wine last night. The alarm woke him at seven o'clock, and after he showered and dressed, he opted for a fried breakfast. It might not be the healthiest option, but one large sandwich isn't enough to keep body and soul together for long. Gus was looking forward to something more substantial tonight. He wondered whether he'd be eating alone.

It was still early. There was plenty of time before leaving to drive to Swindon. He should make it in forty-five minutes unless his old Ford Focus had an off day. He hoped Suzie was out of bed and available to talk. Her drive to work from Worton was shorter, so she shouldn't be leaving for a while yet.

"Good morning," she said, picking up on the fourth ring.

"Did I catch you unawares?" asked Gus.

"Not at all; I just enjoy keeping you on your toes. It doesn't pay to make a man feel you're too eager."

"What are you doing this evening? Do you fancy a meal somewhere?"

"I never reject the offer of a free meal," said Suzie. "What are we celebrating? Surely you haven't solved that new cold case so soon?"

"As if," groaned Gus, "although we may have confirmed that a person who went missing came to a sticky end. Don't ask for details if you've just had breakfast."

"Thanks for the warning. Yes, I had my muesli and yoghurt. But, no doubt, you had a fry-up."

"It's the proper way to start a day," said Gus.

"Not if you want to stay fit and healthy," said Suzie.

"What time tonight?" asked Gus. He thought people were picking on him.

"I'll drive over after work," said Suzie. "We'll wander to the allotments. I enjoy a chat with your old friend, Bert. The vicar might be there too."

"So, the plan is to eat in the Lamb later in the evening, is it?" asked Gus.

"I was buying time to convince you to eat less stodgy food, especially in the summer months. Perhaps we could have a salad?"

"On one condition," said Gus.

"What's that?"

"Neither of us orders a meal with onions or radishes,"

"You know I love you, even though you're quite mad, don't you?"

"I thought of another condition," said Gus. "I'll have as much salad as you want, as long as it comes with steak."

"Incorrigible," said Suzie, "I'll see you at half-past five."

Gus thought he'd got out of that well. He had something to look forward to tonight. So he went outside and set off for Haydon Wick to meet with Jack Sanders.

It made a change to travel alone. As this was a conversation between two former police officers, the rules covering his consultant's role didn't strictly apply. Nevertheless, Gus felt hamstrung when he had to have one team member with him when interviewing a witness or a suspect. He understood the need for the restrictions, but it was different from when he was a serving officer.

Gus realised that Jack Sanders must have retired at around the same time as he had. Neil's notes had informed him that Jack was a widower. They had more in common than he initially thought. As he got closer to the northern suburb of the town, he recalled how Jake Latimer had described the area.

Twenty thousand people were crammed into little boxes. Gus thought that might have been Neil's sour interpretation of what Jake said. His DS wasn't in the best of moods yesterday.

He threaded his way through the sprawling estate with its weird-sounding street names. Whatever happened to Daisy Close and Honeysuckle Mews? Perhaps former councillors had given their names to the signs dotted around every corner.

Gus recalled his conversation with Maggie Burnside yesterday morning, and these street signs were a constant reminder that Swindon boasted forty different nationalities. Finally, Gus drew up outside the semi-detached house where Jack Sander spent his retirement with a few minutes to spare before ten o'clock.

A neatly trimmed privet hedge bordered the house's front garden on three sides. Flowers filled every spare inch of ground that the hedge protected. Oriental poppies, geraniums, violas, irises, and a couple that Gus couldn't name. Maybe one was London Pride, but that sounded more like a brand of bitter, and he might be mistaken.

Gus stared at the plants as he walked up the gravel driveway.

He raised a hand to ring the doorbell.

"I'll be out the back, come on round," said a voice.

Jack Sanders was leaning out of an upstairs window.

The ex-DCI was as brown as a berry. It was plain he spent most of his days in the open air. This front garden didn't get to look this good without effort. Gus wondered what the back garden looked like. He walked along the pathway at the side of the house to find out.

Jack Sanders stood waiting for him. He was taller than Geoff Mercer, but that wasn't difficult. Gus thought Jack was five feet seven or eight, and there was nobody here at number thirty-seven to tell him to eat healthily. The extra weight he was carrying caused Jack to sweat profusely. He mopped his brow with a damp handkerchief as they made their way to the bottom of the garden.

"We'll sit here in the apple trees' shade if that's okay with you?"

"That's fine, Jack," said Gus, "it's Gus, by the way. Our paths never crossed while catching criminals, but I heard plenty of stories."

"The odd good one, I hope?" said Jack. "I heard things about you too when you worked over the other side of the county. How long have you been out?"

"Pretty much the same as you," said Gus, "This garden looks terrific. The flowers at the front and this fruit and vegetable patch at the back are splendid. It must keep you busy?"

"I never had the time when I was working. You know how it is. I got stuck into it after I retired to stop myself from getting bored. Then Avril got diagnosed with pancreatic cancer, and I was on my own eighteen months later. These days, I put the hours in on the garden to take my mind off how much I miss her."

"I lost my wife, Tess, to a brain aneurysm six months after I retired," said Gus. "We'd moved from Salisbury into the countryside to search for the good life. I took on an allotment besides the sizeable garden on the bungalow. Like you, I was alone, and gardening has helped to dull the pain. When you put in the work, the earth gives back in abundance. The colour and beauty of those flowers take your breath away."

Jack and Gus sat in silence for a while as a gentle breeze

rustled the leaves of the trees and a blackbird treated them to a virtuoso performance.

"Some coppers leave all this behind to live in Spain," said Jack Sanders. "Not so bad at this time of year, but in a week or two, it will be a hundred in the shade, and they'll be indoors. Where's the fun in that? What was it you wanted to know, Gus? Anything and everything about that Burnside family?"

"That's about the size of it, Jack," said Gus. "I suppose his murder was one of those cases we get landed with that just won't leave us alone?"

"The ones that keep us awake at night long after we've moved onto a new case. I think I had more than my fair share of those. Grant Burnside wasn't the worst by a long chalk."

"You're kidding," said Gus, "I can't recall you having too many failures."

Jack Sanders laughed and mopped his brow again.

"This will take a while to get the details right. Why don't I fetch us a cold one? A glass of fresh lemon squash, I mean. I don't drink the hard stuff any longer. The doctor's got me under the thumb."

Jack strolled back to the house, and Gus relaxed in his chair. There were worse ways to spend a morning.

Chapter Seven

JACK SANDERS RETURNED with a tray with glasses and a pitcher of lemon squash. He poured them a refreshing drink and then sat back in his chair.

"Right," he said, "did you ever hear about a young lass called Tanya Norris?"

Gus shook his head.

"The name means nothing to me, Jack. Was she someone whose case kept you awake at night because you never cracked it?"

"You're not kidding. It's a while back now, but the more I thought about Grant Burnside's killing in the months after I retired, the more I kept coming back to Tanya Norris."

"Grant's killing was your swan song, wasn't it?" asked Gus.

"It was, and it wasn't the way I would have chosen to leave," said Jack. "A big win was how I wanted to sign off on my career. But, instead, it ended with a whimper. We made zero progress, and the top brass couldn't get me out of the firing line quick enough."

"Typical," said Gus, "they took advantage of you being due to retire to offer up a scapegoat to the press and the public."

"To be fair to them, they waited long enough for the spotlight to have moved on, so my reputation stayed intact."

"What was it about that earlier case that made you think it was like Grant's killing?"

"Way back in 2010, Tanya Norris ran away from her family home in Oxford. Tanya was fifteen. She stayed with a school friend and then drifted from town to town, seeking temporary work. She ended up homeless on the streets in Swindon. Tanya was vulnerable. In only a few weeks, she had been groomed and sold for sex. Tanya's mother had reported her missing, but we had few resources available to find a delinquent teenager. There were four men believed to have carried out the grooming and abuse. They were two sets of brothers who preyed on pre-teen and underage teenage girls. Rumours started in 2005 that something was happening here, matching events in Oxford and several northern cities."

"It was becoming a familiar pattern across the country back then," said Gus. "Most of those men came from Muslim backgrounds. Their victims were nearly always white. People who suspected criminal activity contacted the authorities, but nobody followed it up because they feared getting accused of racism. As most of these girls were from broken homes, it was easier to dismiss their stories as being made up purely to get sympathy. The authorities discounted the rumours and complaints as unreliable."

"Hindsight's a wonderful thing," said Sanders. "In the Spring of 2012, Tanya Norris became pregnant. She arrived distressed outside the doors of the Great Western Hospital on Marlborough Road. Tanya claimed the gang had attempted to make her miscarry. Doctors treated her, and as she recovered, they listened to Tanya's claims of what she'd suffered for the past two years. What happened next was the first strange occurrence. Tanya left the hospital with a couple claiming to be her parents. After that, she hasn't been heard of again."

"Did anyone get statements from the medical staff who treated Tanya Norris?" asked Gus. "Did you have details of how this grooming gang operated?"

"Yes," replied Sanders, "after initial contact on the streets or a local park, the girls were taken to various events, travelled around town in top-of-the-range cars, and received presents. The men lulled the girls into believing they cared for them. It was easy to see why. They never had much love at home. For a few, it was the first time anyone had shown them affection. After giving them free access to alcohol, the next step was to offer them drugs, and Tanya and the others soon became dependent on the gang. That was when the nightmare began. After the four men had used and abused the girls for several days, they set them to work at various addresses around the town where dozens of men paid to have sex with them."

"Today, there are at least seventy-five towns and cities in the UK where grooming gangs operate," said Gus. "Eight years ago, we imagined Rochdale and Oxford were isolated examples. However, the problem went far deeper than anyone dreamed. Who was responsible for things here in Swindon?"

"Anjum and Kamal Ahmed, and Farhan and Bassam Hussein were in their early to mid-thirties. The brothers believed young white girls were naturally promiscuous because they were non-believers, non-Muslims. They deserved to be exploited and degraded. The Hussein brothers drove around town in a brand-new Lexus. We found CCTV evidence of them on Queen's Drive, travelling towards the A419, on an evening in late January 2012. It's believed they were ferrying girls from a nightclub in Old Town back to the flats where the girls stayed. The Lexus returned an hour later but turned off the main road onto one of the many side streets without camera coverage. The brothers' car was abandoned on a side street in Rodbourne the following morning. It was locked and empty. Neither brother was ever heard from again."

Jack Sanders topped up their glasses and then continued his grim tale.

"Anjum Ahmed drove a BMW and was the typical young driver who ignored the rules of the road. After leaving the nightclub, the Ahmed brothers' route appeared to lead them to Toothill. Again, they appeared on CCTV. It was easy to spot Anjum. He darted from lane to lane, looking for an opportunity to put his foot down. As often as he did that, he needed to brake with equal ferocity. After thirty minutes, we spotted them returning from the outskirts and thought they were heading home through Old Town. We assumed that the Porsche 911 behind them was already racing the BMW. Because at the Mead Way roundabout, the two cars shot off on the A419 towards Blunsdon."

"You couldn't identify where this Porsche and the BMW first made contact?"

"No, it must have been in the suburbs somewhere."

"Was the driver of the 911 known to the police?" asked Gus.

"The car was registered to a private company. There was no way to know who might have been driving it that night. Thirty minutes later, the Porsche returned alone, travelling within the speed limit, and turned towards Old

Town. We began receiving phone calls about the burned-out BMW in the morning."

"Let me guess," said Gus, "there was no sign of the Ahmed brothers."

"Not after that sighting at Mead Way."

"How did you explain that?" asked Gus.

"You may know that the Burnside gang were building their empire," said Sanders, "and people like Edwards and Franchetti had people operating in the town. Either of those three outfits could have been responsible, but they were only interested in the drugs. The Burnside gang have never stooped to trafficking young girls for sex."

"They see themselves as proper villains brought up to respect family values, I suppose?"

Sanders smiled.

"Something like that. Either way, that particular grooming gang ceased to be a problem. We don't know what happened to the young girls. But the word on the streets was that several flats and rooms in private houses became available in February that year."

"It sounds too public-spirited to me for the Burnsides or one of the other gangs to get involved," said Gus. "Did anyone dig deeper to learn what was behind it?"

"We had enough on our plates," sighed Sanders, "apart from a rising crime rate. The Olympics was only a few months away. You know what it's like if the problem goes away without you needing to take action, you move on to something where you can best utilise your resources."

"Why did the Grant Burnside murder get you thinking about Tanya Norris?" asked Gus.

"Two sets of brothers disappear without a trace. Someone eliminates the grooming gang they operate, and the girls are missing. Four years later, one of our most notorious gang leaders gets shot dead, and once again, there's not a single clue to follow. Something strange was behind it. I'm certain of it. You get a niggle, don't you, and it doesn't go away?"

"I get those niggles too, Jack," said Gus, "maybe you're right, and there was something odd."

Gus thought Colonel Jack Sanders had helped him as much as he could. It was time to leave the retired DCI to his gardening. Gus thanked Jack for the lemon squash, said his goodbyes and walked back to his car. He sat with the key poised for a while and reviewed the latter part of their conversation. Sometimes an investigation throws up more questions than answers. Gus couldn't stop thinking about the fate of the poor girls.

According to Jack Sanders, the young girls disappeared in early 2012. That change in their circumstances occurred within days of the disappearance of the two pairs of brothers. They were the men responsible for grooming the girls, selling their bodies to all, and sundry across Swindon over at least two years. So where did the girls go? Who took them, and why? Jack Sanders said that someone took Tanya Norris away too. Did someone kill her and dispose of the body to ensure her silence? It wasn't unheard of, and killers did it all the time. But what of the others? Surely, a number between twelve and twenty was impossible to keep hidden?

Suppose those poor girls were still alive, Gus thought. They would be between nineteen and twenty-three now. They should be in proper jobs, have formed relationships, and get married and have children at that age. He kept coming back to who took them and why? Gus didn't want to think about that too much.

While they were in their early teens, they were a valuable commodity. Could other grooming gangs around the country have absorbed these girls into their numbers? That wasn't such a fanciful idea. Instances of girls from Liverpool and Manchester getting trafficked to Birmingham and Bristol were commonplace. Most were addicted to drugs and had given up hope of escaping long ago. The drugs were what they craved, and hopefully, the dosage the gangs gave them was strong enough to shut out the horrors of what happened to them every day.

How could he find out the fate of these girls? Who would know their names? Apart from Tanya Norris, they were a mystery. Gus pondered for a while. But, no, the Burnside murder must come first.

Gus didn't share Jack's niggle about any connection between the cases. How could they be? A professional hitman shot Grant; that was clear. Were the four brothers even dead? Could there be a more straightforward explanation for their disappearance?

The only way Gus could see the cases being linked was if there was an unseen hand. Someone was dispensing swift justice wherever they thought criminals weren't getting identified and charged by the police. That was as unlikely as Swindon Town winning the Premiership, to use one of Neil's analogies.

Maybe later, he'd chat with Geoff Mercer over a pint and explore the fate of the Ahmed and Hussein brothers. They were no loss. But, same as the girls, they suddenly disappeared with no explanation. Jack's case involving Tanya Norris was as challenging to understand as who murdered Grant Burnside.

Gus started the car and drove back to the Old Police Station. Perhaps a debrief with the rest of the team, and a revised interview schedule would give them a fresh start. They certainly needed it.

"I hope you've kept busy while I was in Haydon Wick?" he asked as soon as he entered the office.

"It's been tough with no interviews, guv," said Neil, "but our filing is bang up to date, and I gave the restroom a spring clean."

"Each of us could use a spring clean now and again," said Gus, "is everything else sorted now?"

"Yes, guv," said Neil.

Luke and Lydia shared a glance. Did that have to do with Neil's early finish yesterday? They had learned nothing from Neil this morning.

"What did you two find to do?" asked Gus.

"A general tidy up out here, guv," said Lydia, "and I took a phone call from London Road."

"Not bad news, I hope. I don't want to drive there this afternoon."

"No, guv," said Lydia, "it was DS Mercer. He told us that your office furniture would arrive on Friday at two o'clock. Three desks, two chairs, and two filing cabinets. With Alex returning to work and DC Umeh joining us, we must re-arrange the layout of the office."

"Well, it's a start," said Gus. "Did he offer us any laptops or printers while he was having a clear-out from his suite of offices?"

"I compiled a comprehensive list of stationery items, guv," said Luke, "I waited until you got back to check it before sending it through to London Road."

"You know best what we'll be short of when our numbers increase next month, Luke. Just make sure we have enough coffee and biscuits. Our budget's tight, or so the ACC kept telling me when we started. He'll cut corners wherever he can. Add in two high-priced items that would only be a luxury. Truelove can take great pleasure in crossing them off the list, and perhaps we'll get one hundred per cent of the basics."

"What did you hear in Haydon Wick, guv?" asked Neil.

"I heard a blast from the past, Neil," said Gus.

"Andy Partridge and XTC, guv?" asked Neil.

Gus wondered about the level of Neil's musical taste, not for the first time.

"Far more chilling than that, Neil. A Swindon grooming gang was erased from the scene without troubling our people at Gablecross back in 2012. Jack Sanders thought it suspicious. So suspicious that when Grant Burnside died at the hands of a mystery man, he imagined it could be the responsibility of the same people."

"Do you think there's anything in that, guv?" asked Luke.

"I can't see it, Luke."

"Was that everything then, guv?" asked Neil.

Gus had to admit it was the sum of what he'd learned from Jack Sanders this morning.

"Do we revise our schedule now, guv?" asked Luke.

"We'll start with Henry Burnside," said Gus. "I want you and Neil to take him. Ask what happened to Howard Todd after you've got him to confirm Todd worked for him. Since Gary Burnside insists they are a legitimate import-export company, I want to know what work Henry could offer him."

"What work did the drug dealer, Howard Todd, carry out for you, Mr Burnside?" said Neil.

"Henry will have Patrick Iverson hovering on his shoulder. So you might want to re-phrase that, but that's the gist. Press Henry on who he thought killed his father. Try to needle him, without getting Iverson too excited, by hinting at differences between the three brothers."

"We're to imply that we've heard rumours somebody wanted Grant out. Either for the three brothers to gain control or, in Henry's case, because he didn't want to work for Gary."

"We'll be doing something similar when we speak with Joseph. Divide and conquer. That could be the way to go. Get them riled, and force them to react. Of course, Iverson will do everything he can to keep a lid on their tempers, but it's their default position. As natural as for Lydia to smile."

"Will you and I interview Joseph Burnside?" asked the smiling Lydia.

"Not at the same time because Iverson will want to be in attendance. Luke, it would be best if you used similar tactics for Joseph. He will deflect your question on Todd, as Gary did yesterday. But pursue the family friction angle. Lydia. I'm going to ask you to come to HMP Bristol with me. You can refuse if you wish. Vic Hodge is a nasty piece of work."

"I'll cope," said Lydia. "Do I need to wear any particular style of clothing?"

"Don't ask, Luke," said Neil.

"I picked up the odd vibe while you were on leave, Neil," said Luke, "those tactics would be wasted on me."

"Smart and professional, Lydia," said Gus. "Nothing provocative required tomorrow."

"When do we start these interviews, guv?" asked Neil.

"First thing tomorrow for Henry. You two can carry straight through with Joseph if he's available. Iverson will probably persuade Joseph to alter his plans to save having to disrupt his busy day twice. Lydia and I will make arrangements this afternoon for a visit to Horfield. When we return tomorrow afternoon, we'll visit Kerry Burnside. She lives alone, I believe, at the registered address of the so-called company offices."

"Yes, guv," said Lydia, "Kerry lives in an upstairs flat with her dogs, while the ground floor is now modern office space."

"I'll push tomorrow's original interviews back twenty-four hours, guv," said Luke,

"Cancel Sylvia Kerr altogether," said Gus, "as for Andy Wilkinson, I think we can tell him we'll drop by his unit for a chat if it proves necessary. I might ask him to look at my Focus while we're there."

"You're taking a huge risk, guv," said Neil, "He does car repairs. Not the impossible. Wilkinson might give your old banger the last rites."

"Hilarious, Neil. Unless he saw the sniper, Wilkinson won't be much help, anyway. As for Howard's sister Amanda, as his body will never get found, we can't do a thing for her. We need a signed confession before getting Gablecross to send a uniform round to Mandy to notify her of his death. Otherwise, the poor woman will have to wait another three years until Howard's been missing for seven."

"That just leaves Fergus McHugh," said Luke.

"Just the three of us need to go on that trip," said Gus. "Make sure we've got boots, masks and those natty blue suits in the car's boot. It could get messy."

"Thanks, guv," said Lydia, "I got squeamish when my Dad had to bury my pet rabbit, Fluffy. So I appreciate giving that trip a miss."

"Right, let's crack on with adjusting our timetables for tomorrow. Remember, when making those calls, remind whoever you're contacting that if they mess us around, I'll contact Gablecross and make it official. Then, they can attend the custody suite under caution."

"Yes, guv," replied Luke and Neil. So Gus called HMP Bristol to discover whether Vic Hodge was up for visitors.

He met no resistance, and he and Lydia had their ten o'clock meeting confirmed with one of the Burnsides' enforcers.

"Hodge was happy to oblige, guv?" asked Lydia.

"The warden told me Vic had nothing on his social calendar for tomorrow."

During the last few minutes before the end of play at five o'clock, Gus sketched an office layout from the second of July on one of the whiteboards.

"Leave that there for two days," he said as he was heading for the lift, "if you can think of a better solution, we'll discuss it Friday lunchtime."

WHILE GUS DROVE HOME to Urchfont, he went through the day's events. But were they even on the right track? Nothing they had heard in the first two full days of this cold case review suggested a clear route to follow. Unless they miraculously unearthed a hidden clue that unlocked the mystery surrounding Grant Burnside's death, then this could be a lost cause.

Gus wondered what joys tomorrow might bring. The brothers would be tight-lipped under Iverson's eagle eye. Vic Hodge and Kerry Burnside were at opposite ends of the intelligence spectrum, and neither was a likely candidate for Grant's killer.

What else was there? They could spend five minutes jogging Andy Wilkinson's memories of a Sunday morning four years ago. In case he saw Chuck Norris, but it had slipped his mind.

As for Farmer McHugh, Gus's conjecture that Fergus helped the Burnside gang dispose of bodies for over a decade was just that, conjecture. If that sodium hydroxide method worked as effectively as McHugh claimed, then any evidence had gone.

Gus sighed as he drove through the gateway from the lane and parked the car. What he needed was a pleasant summer evening in company. It was the ideal way to let everything wash over him and help him forget the case for a few precious hours.

Thank goodness he'd called Suzie first thing. Another thirty minutes, and she should park her GTI beside his Focus. Gus opened the front door and walked into the hallway. He stooped to retrieve a handful of mail secured with an elastic band.

Gus groaned when he recognised the messages on several of the contents. Every political party was keen to remind each household of their opinions on Brexit. As if everyone had been in a coma for the past two years. There was even an invitation to attend a mass rally in London on Saturday. Gus was confident he had a previous engagement.

Six out of the eight items soon headed into the box for recycling. Gus glanced at the Electoral Roll reminder and wondered whether the details for the bungalow would change before the next election. The way things were going, it could change in weeks, not years.

Gus turned the final item over to check the address. It was rare to receive an envelope of quality, even on his birthday. Who could be writing to him? The handwriting was old-school and extremely neat. The postmark was faded, but unmistakably this was a letter from France. Gus hadn't seen one of those for a while.

I hope you are well. After the trial, my sons brought me to the chateau to make a new life. Crompton accompanied me. I couldn't be without the old devil. I wanted you to know that I never blamed you for what you did. The truth had to come out.

You were so kind to me the last time we spoke. You feared I might fly to the bottle again and drink myself to death. But I must say, I enjoy our wine, and 2017 might be a vintage you should stock in your cellar (if you have one, silly me).

The boys ensure I keep things under control, and the food and weather are divine.

I thank God every day for this second chance at life, but most of all—I thank you, Freeman. Bless you.

Joyce

Gus heard the key in the door behind him. Suzie was early.

"Hello you," she said.

"You won't guess who this letter came from," said Gus.

Suzie read Joyce Pemberton-Smythe's letter.

"Aw, bless her. She's a good sort, isn't she?"

"I've never received a pleasant letter from the wife of a murderer before," said Gus, "I've had the odd death threat from people I've nicked and their families, of course. It goes with the territory."

"You should frame this and hang it on the wall in the office," said Suzie. "Was this the high point of your day?"

"Without a doubt," said Gus, "the latest case is like swimming in treacle. I don't want to hear it mentioned again tonight. Let's decide where we're going to eat."

"I hoped we would visit your allotment first," said Suzie. "I've got an old pair of jeans and a t-shirt in the wardrobe.

Why don't you shower and change? Alone, or we'll get nothing done. I'll be ready to leave when you're finished."

Gus decided it was best to follow orders on this occasion. So, fifteen minutes later, they were striding towards the old church and the gateway into the allotments. As soon as they turned the corner, they spotted Bert Penman and Clemency Bentham hard at work.

"A fine evening for it, Mr Freeman," said Bert, straightening up from gathering his early potatoes.

Gus wondered whether Irene North would find half of those on her doorstep later.

"Have you been at it long, Mr Penman?" asked Suzie.

"All my life, Miss, and the gardening," said Bert.

The Reverend tutted. She came across to speak with Gus.

"He's putting on a brave front," said Clemency. "The events of the past two weeks have hit him hard. But, that patch of ground is his best hope of returning to his old self."

"I can see that you've both made excellent progress since my last visit," said Gus.

"I spent half an hour helping you out, Mr Freeman," said Bert. "Now you've got young Suzie Ferris with you. I shall expect to see things getting back on track."

"My first job is to root around in that shed of mine to find those notes you gave me," said Gus, "I don't know what I'm doing without them. Are you two staying long?"

"I can hear a pint of cider calling me from the Lamb," said Bert. "If I behave myself, the Reverend said she'd join me when that church clock strikes seven."

"Have you both eaten?" asked Gus, "Suzie and I would welcome the company."

"That would be splendid," said Clemency. "My diet

dictates that I only order a child's portion of salad, but I can watch you three devour something more edible."

"I had a meal at lunchtime," said Bert, "but as the Reverend says, there's plenty on the menu for those who only require a snack."

"That's settled then," said Suzie, "we'll hunt for whatever Gus has mislaid and then catch up with you in the Lamb. We'll be no later than half-past seven."

Gus and Suzie left Bert and Clemency to do their chores. Gus opened his old shed and ventured inside. Suzie joined him and helped turn over seedboxes, catalogues, and gardening gloves.

"Here we are," cried Gus, "I can't think why I didn't check here before. I tucked it into my Kierkegaard book to mark a comment I'd scribbled on a well-loved page.

Gus handed the book to Suzie. She read the written comment aloud.

"Life is what happens when you're getting ready for something else - Gus Freeman."

"Oh, you fancy yourself as a philosopher now, do you?" grinned Suzie, "I'm sure someone coined that phrase already."

"Maybe," said Gus, "but I thought it apposite at the time."

"Did I inspire you to commit your inner feelings to paper?" asked Suzie, putting her arms around him and kissing him deeply.

"If you keep this up, we're going to need a bigger shed," said Gus.

"Don't worry," said Suzie, "we'll have plenty of time once I'm living in the village full-time."

The church clock gathered itself to chime the hour.

"You've decided then?" Gus asked.

The clock struck seven times while they kissed.

"Pretty much," said Suzie when they came up for air.

When they emerged from the shed, Clemency and Bert had gone.

"Thirty minutes to do everything in these notes for the final weeks in June," sighed Gus. "We'll only scratch the surface."

"Pick one task each, get stuck in and quit moaning," said Suzie. "The exercise will sharpen your appetite."

Gus couldn't argue with the logic, so they set to and walked up the lane to the Lamb at seven-thirty. They found Bert and Clemency seated at a table in the beer garden.

"I hesitate to ask," said Gus, "but are you ready for another drink?"

"Not for me, Gus," said Clemency, "this elderflower cordial will last me the whole evening."

Bert's pint glass was already on its way to his lips.

"Just a toothful left in this first one, Mr Freeman. You're a gentleman."

Suzie had fetched menus from inside the pub. Gus went to order drinks while the others decided what they were eating. Suzie passed him with the menus as he returned with a tray.

"Don't I get a chance to see what's on offer?" he asked.

"I'll order you steak, chips, and salad; without the chips," she grinned.

Gus groaned.

"Bert's got news for you, Gus," said Clemency.

"My daughter, Margaret, arrives next Friday," said Bert. "Her husband has flown back to New Zealand to care for his business interests. Brett, my grandson, will accompany

Margaret. I don't know yet how long they're staying. After that, Margaret needs to fly home. Brett's using this visit to check out job opportunities. Then, if he can find something that suits his qualifications and experience, he'll move to the UK for good."

"Where will they stay?" asked Gus.

"Lucknam Park Manor Hotel, Colerne," said Bert.

"Very swish," said Suzie, who had rejoined them.

"Brett will hire a car, and that hotel is an excellent base for visiting Bath and anywhere in Wiltshire."

Gus listened to Bert, Clemency, and Suzie chatting about the potential visits that Bert's daughter and grandson might enjoy. When the food arrived at their table, he tucked into his steak. An evening like this was just what was needed. A few chips would have helped, but good company and the pub's warm ambience helped him relax at last.

His mind was clear. After a good night's sleep, he would enter the fray with renewed vigour. The answer to Grant's murder was there somewhere. Unfortunately, they weren't looking in the right place yet.

Chapter Eight

Thursday, 21 June 2018

GUS DIDN'T NEED the alarm in the morning. Suzie dug him in the ribs at half-past seven.

"Rise and shine," she said, "I need to drive home before I go to work."

Gus padded silently into the bathroom. He showered and dressed, then wandered into the kitchen to find that Suzie had already eaten. She emerged from the bedroom wearing his pink shirt as he searched for bacon and eggs in the fridge.

It still looked better on her than it ever had on him.

"My turn in the shower," she said. "A fry-up. Are you sure that's wise?"

"It may not be wise, but I need it after a heavy night out."

"That's your fault for trying to match Bert Penman, drink for drink. That man has hollow legs. Bert's unlike any eighty-five-year-old I've ever known."

"How many have you known?"

"None, in the biblical sense. Not that it's any of your business. Other than that, perhaps two. Where are you off to today?"

"HMP Bristol," said Gus, "just visiting with Lydia."

"Have fun. I'll see you tomorrow night at around six. Is that okay?"

"Perfect. Take that shower, or you'll be late on parade."

Gus restricted himself to one egg and two rashers of bacon. Then, in the interests of balance, he drank two large mugs of black coffee. He wasn't ready for anything but as close as he had any right to be.

When Suzie returned, glowing and full of youthful exuberance, Gus wondered how lucky he'd gotten. They clung to one another for several seconds before she pulled away to look at him.

"Will we still be like this if I'm here all the time," she said, "or is this only because we won't see one another for thirty-six hours?"

"An interesting question," said Gus. "I shall have to give it a good deal of thought and deliver my philosophical wisdom on the matter tomorrow evening."

"You say today is merely a visit to Horfield?" asked Suzie as she stood by the front door. "You're mad; perhaps Lydia should leave you there."

Gus listened to Suzie's car repositioning the gravel on the driveway and putting their breakfast things in the dishwasher. He was collecting Lydia on the way to Bristol, so he needn't leave for another forty minutes. Gus tried to remember whether he had a picture frame lying idle in the house for Joyce's letter.

"DS SHERMAN and DS Davis to see DI Trefor Davies," said Luke as he and Neil arrived at Marlborough Police Station for the first of today's interviews.

"There's a Jaguar in the car park," said Neil. "I bet that's the oily solicitor's."

"Iverson can wait. We're okay for time," said Luke, "ah, here comes Trefor Davies now."

"Good morning, lads," said Trefor, "your victim awaits. Burnside has his minder with him, so stay sharp."

Luke and Neil followed Trefor Davies along the corridor and entered the room.

Henry Burnside didn't look up from whatever interested him on the carpeted floor. Patrick Iverson checked his watch. He needn't have bothered. The wall clock in front of him read nine o'clock precisely.

"Thank you for attending this morning, Henry," said Luke, "I don't believe we've met. I'm DS Luke Sherman, and my colleague is DS Neil Davis. We work with a Crime Review Team looking into your father's murder in 2014. I wouldn't be surprised if we didn't find his killer this time. We've chatted with three members of your family so far, and everyone's been most helpful."

Henry looked up when he heard that comment.

"What have they been saying about me?" he asked.

"I don't think your name cropped up that often from the reports I've read," said Neil.

"Davis, was it?" asked Henry. "Did your father get himself killed a few weeks back? We've got that in common, then. It hurts, doesn't it? Especially when the coppers never gave a toss about finding out who did it for four years."

Iverson gave a polite cough.

"Stick to the narrative, gentlemen. You know very well

that the conversations you've had to date have produced nothing of any significance."

"Can you confirm your whereabouts on Sunday the twenty-fifth of May in 2014?" asked Luke, "between the hours of six in the morning and noon."

"The same place I told the coppers the day after my father got shot," said Henry.

"Did you ever have cause to visit the unit on the Cheney Manor Industrial Estate as part of your role in the family, um, import-export business?"

"I went there, yeah, so what? We don't use it anymore."

Luke studied Henry Burnside. He was three inches shorter than Gary, two years younger, but as much as two stones lighter. The shaved head and tattooed neck were an attempt to make him appear more menacing. But instead, it only made Henry seem scrawny and scruffy.

Yesterday, Gary, his elder brother, dressed smartly and casually. You could easily get fooled into thinking he was an honest citizen, even if his gold accessories were over the top. You couldn't do otherwise than think Henry was a wannabe thug.

"Where do you carry out the punishment beatings these days then, Henry?" asked Luke.

"That might have gone on in Dad's days," said Henry, "I'm not saying they did. We run a legitimate business now."

"Do you remember when Blake Dixon died at the snooker club?" asked Neil.

"Of course, it was in the papers. Dad got accused of that, but it was rubbish."

"Grant used that club a lot, didn't he?" asked Neil.

"We all did," said Henry, "Gary still does."

"If you needed to teach someone a lesson, like Howard

Todd, after the snooker club got too risky, where would you do that?" asked Neil.

"Toddy moved out of the area," said Henry, "and never left a forwarding address. So Kerry's still got holiday pay in an account for him."

"Did you know he was a drug dealer when you took him on?" asked Neil.

"Grant Burnside was an equal opportunities employer," said Iverson. "Gary told you yesterday how the family always had to fight for everything they achieved. So Grant felt it only right to offer Mr Todd a helping hand."

"You're very strong on the family, aren't you, Henry?" said Luke. "Didn't you ever itch to be top dog? You had Grant shouting the orders when you started, and we know he was a hard taskmaster. As soon as he's dead, Gary takes his place. Did you wonder about that? Could Gary have wanted to move things along more quickly?"

"You're a nut job," said Henry, "probably an only child. Family is everything. We stick together, no matter what. Dad would have carried on until he thought it was time to pass the baton. Nobody would have tried to get him to step aside. Gary is the eldest, and it stands to reason that he would take over. There was no question about it. No argument. Nothing can tear us apart. You can try to spread seeds of doubt as much as you like, but you're wasting your breath. Now, if there's nothing else, I've got a business to run."

"One last question, Henry," said Neil. "If none of the Burnside family did it, nor any of the enemies you checked for yourselves, then who do you think killed your father?"

"That's what you reckoned was your job. The first thing I heard when we got here," said Henry, shrugging a shoulder. "If you get a name, you better keep it close to your chest because if word gets out, I won't give them great odds of lasting twenty-four hours."

"Our boss is visiting Vic Hodge about now," said Luke. "Perhaps he knows where you rented the replacement warehouse space."

"Vic's a good soldier," said Henry, "he and Gary grew up together. So Vic won't tell you anything."

"Vic hasn't got Denver Drewett there to remind him what to say," said Luke, "and Mr Iverson's here with us this morning. Vic isn't the brightest, and Gus Freeman can be very persuasive. We can't help Denver. He's in the wind, but we can help Vic Hodge. I wonder what deal might be on the table?"

"The same thing applies. I'd give Vic twenty-four hours," said Henry Burnside.

"I still represent Mr Hodge when asked," said Iverson. "Why didn't you inform me you were seeing him this morning?"

"No comment," said Luke.

Henry Burnside got up and walked out. Iverson followed him. Joseph Burnside would be in Reception waiting to come through.

As soon as they were alone, Luke and Neil did a quick high-five.

"I wanted to say that. Did you see Iverson's face?" said Neil.

"Yes," said Luke, "but we didn't get much more than confirmation that Todd was supposedly an employee."

"I pressed him on the gang using the snooker club, too," said Neil. "Gary spent more time there than the others. I didn't get the impression Henry spent much time with Gary since Grant's death."

"Another few minutes and Joseph will be here. We'll ask

him the same questions unless you can think of anything else we could try?"

"Do you reckon Gus wants to hear what Henry had to say? I could send a text to Lydia with the highlights. It might prove handy when they're chatting to Hodge."

"It can't hurt, Neil," said Luke. "If you're going to do it, get on with it. Iverson and Joseph Burnside are already outside in the corridor. Joseph's receiving his final briefing."

Neil composed a quick text and sent it to Lydia.

"I THOUGHT Horfield would be a depressing place, with the prison being the major reason for people recognising the name," said Lydia, "but it's attractive, isn't it?"

"I believe it's become one of the most in-demand places to live in Bristol," said Gus. "That's because of the A38 Gloucester Road running through the middle, and the independent shops, bars, and restaurants that line either side."

Gus had allowed sufficient time to negotiate security at HMP Bristol. Vic Hodge was one of around seven hundred Category B prisoners housed there. A few minutes before ten, a prison officer escorted Gus and Lydia to the interview room.

"Hang on, I've got a text message, guv," said Lydia, fishing around in her bag for her phone when she heard it buzz.

"Check it quickly, and then turn it off," said Gus.

"It's from Neil. You had better read it."

Vic Hodge arrived outside the door on the dot of ten. He was a giant of a man. Lydia was glad there would be a large table between them. Gus continued to read the message as a warder led the prisoner into the room.

Hodge sat on the metal chair and studied the two faces opposite.

Hodge's escort and the prison officer stood against the back wall.

"Thank you for agreeing to meet us today, Vic," said Gus, handing Lydia her phone. "You don't mind if I call you Vic, I hope?"

"It doesn't bother me," Hodge replied.

"My name is Freeman, I'm a consultant with Wiltshire Police, and we're taking a fresh look into your old boss's murder. Do you remember that day, Vic?"

"I'm hardly likely to forget, am I?" muttered Hodge

"What were you doing that morning?" asked Gus.

"Grant wanted us to work for him out at the warehouse."

"You're serving a sentence for demanding money with menaces," said Gus. "What type of work might Grant want you for, I wonder?"

"It's four years ago now. I can't remember," said Vic.

"Did you ever visit the snooker club with Grant?"

"We went there often enough," said Vic. "Gary liked to play. That wasn't my thing."

"Have you heard from your old mate, Denver, since you've been here?" asked Gus.

"I haven't heard a word from Denver since I got nicked."

"No, Denver did a runner, didn't he? Your mate left you to face the music. You were carrying a gun that day, and they threw the book at you. Gary and his brothers kept their distance, didn't they? There was no way they were getting dragged down with you. Would it interest you to know that Henry and Joseph are speaking with my colleagues right now? Mr Iverson is holding their hand, making sure they don't come to harm. Meanwhile, you're here alone. Odd that, isn't it, Vic? The Burnsides are always so passionate about the family unit. I bet you and Denver got told you were family too. Each of you was surrounded by a protective shield. Iverson was always on hand. He was there to tell you the best course of action that Sunday morning, wasn't he?"

"Mr Iverson was there; yeah, Gary didn't know what to do."

"It was a difficult problem, I'll grant you that," said Gus, sitting back in his chair.

Lydia wondered where he was going with this. Neil's text had told them nothing, yet he had a big grin as he handed her back her phone.

"I forgot to mention that we spoke to Gary yesterday afternoon. Sorry. We know why Grant asked for your help at the unit out at Cheney Manor. Howard Todd had crossed the line, and an example had to be made. You, Denver, and Gary looked for him, found where he was hiding, and Grant picked you up in the Mercedes. Using the snooker club after that messy business with Blake Dixon was too risky. So, you started using the quiet unit at the back of the Cheney Manor site when a punishment beating was necessary. Only, with Toddy, it was way past that, wasn't it? He had to disappear for good. After it was over, Grant delivered Toddy to McHugh, and you and Denver had to clean up the mess. When they got back, Grant got shot, and Gary called Iverson. What did he tell you? Keep the doors shut. Don't let the cops inside. Tell them you just arrived. Then Gary rang for the police and the ambulance. Have we got everything right, Vic? Anything you think we've missed?"

Vic sat quietly for at least two minutes while Gus let him think things over. He could almost see the cogs turning.

Lydia realised that Gus had pieced the scraps of information they had gathered to concoct a plausible scenario. It sounded believable, the way he explained it. Could they prove it in a court of law, though? Were Gus's assumptions even correct? Why hadn't Vic already accused Gus of fishing if they weren't? Lydia expected Hodge to deny involvement or reply 'no comment' to everything. But, instead, Hodge had just kept staring at the table and let Gus ramble on with his hypothesis.

Vic looked up, and Gus could see in his eyes that the man had resigned himself to his fate. The gamble had succeeded.

"I can't believe they told you that much," said Vic, "not with Iverson there to do what they pay him to do. Kerry was right. He's a snake. We should both have gotten out sooner. There's no chance of that now."

That was different, Gus thought. Nobody mentioned Kerry Burnside and Vic Hodge in the same sentence before.

"Do you get many visitors, Vic?" he asked.

"Kerry comes every week when she can. Nobody else has been near the place,"

"How long have you and Kerry been together?" asked Lydia.

Vic gave her a wry smile.

"It's not like that. Neither of us ever had anybody. Look at me. I never had a hope in hell with the plain girls I met, let alone someone as pretty as you. Gary and the others made fun of Kerry because of how she looked. There was no way we could have seen one another. Gary would have made our lives miserable. After I got sent to prison for this stretch, Kerry wrote and asked if she could visit. The longer everything went on after Grant died, the more we realised it was wrong."

Gus left that for a while. He was unsure what had gone on after Grant died, apart from the increased reliance of the gang on the drugs trade. Grant's traditional robberies were history after he died. Everything centred on trafficking and dealing. Was that what Vic meant? Gus tried another tactic to get Vic talking. Now he'd started, the floodgates might open.

"How did you get involved in crime in the first place," asked Gus. "You were at school with Gary, weren't you?"

"Yeah, when I was growing up, I watched the older boys doing well, making money, driving flash cars and that, you know? They were all doing gangster stuff. By the time I was eleven, I was thieving and selling drugs alongside Gary and Denver. It was only a short step to carrying a weapon. Denver had a knife, so I got one. I didn't enjoy that way of life, and anyone who tells you they do is a liar. You're waiting for your door to get kicked in. It could be the law, or it could be guys from another gang. Either way, it spells trouble. Look at me now. I'm forty next year with three prison stints, including this one. They charged me with demanding money with menaces. I asked for the money. Okay, perhaps I shouted, but the gun did for me. Why did I carry it? It was purely for protection. I never wanted to have to use it. After taking it with me for a few months, I forgot I had it. It was second nature to stick it in my pocket. I'd check I had everything before I left home—keys, wallet, watch, gun. How stupid is that?"

"It's always about choices, Vic," said Gus, "when did the Burnsides take you on?"

"By the time I was eighteen, I was as big as a house and strong with it. Gary used Denver and me for our muscles. We waded in when any trouble started, and we managed it with our fists nine times out of ten. We also put the occasional boot in when people didn't stay on the floor. Gary asked Denver and me to join the firm because Henry and Joseph were useless in a fight. They never got involved in any rough stuff. If someone was out of line, they passed the word to Grant, and he told Gary to sort it. Gary called us in to put the frighteners on people. That's it. We weren't killers, Mr Freeman. That's the truth."

"You both worked for Gary in 2009 when Spencer Curtis died," asked Gus.

"Yeah, Grant wanted him dead. So Gary told Denver and me to find Curtis and take him to them. They were waiting for us in a car at Blacklands, near Calne. We used the firm's old van that night. We didn't have the Mercedes in those days; it was a white Ford Transit. We dropped Curtis on the ground, wrapped him in plastic sheeting, and drove away. First thing next morning, Denver told me Gary had called him and said to make an anonymous call to the police, telling them where to find the body."

"The Burnsides were happy to risk you and Denver getting caught but distanced themselves from the sharp end," said Gus. "Not such a tight family, after all, were you?"

Vic Hodge didn't reply.

"You were present the night Blake Dixon died too," Gus said.

"We took him to the snooker club, into the Matchroom, where Gary likes to go."

"What's the Matchroom?" asked Gus.

"A private room with one table for the tournament

matches, money games, etc. The cloth they put on is super-fast, the same as at The Crucible for the professionals. In the old days, the pros visited the club to play exhibitions. They don't come anymore."

"How many tables are there altogether?" asked Gus.

"They've got a mixture of snooker and pool tables these days. I'm not sure. Back then, there were seven snooker tables in the main room. It wasn't easy to get more in because of the concrete pillars. The staff had cameras behind the bar for the outside tables to see what was happening. Grant didn't mind the odd deal getting done, but when the lads brought their girlfriends, you can imagine what went on in the dark corners."

"What happened that night with Blake Dixon?" asked Gus.

"Grant and Gary took him into the Matchroom. Denver and I had given him a hiding before we brought him inside. We stood guard outside the door, thinking the place was empty. We couldn't see the lads playing on Table 7 because of the pillars. They were racking the balls up for a new frame, and one had gone for a fag. All hell broke loose when the shotgun went off, and the lads dashed for the door. Denver told them to stay put and keep their mouth shut. Grant came out of the room and realised someone had been there. He was an arrogant sod, as always. Grant reckoned he was untouchable, so he just told the bar manager to give the lads a beer and put their table fees on his tab. They got the message they were dead if he heard they ever said a word."

"What about Howard Todd?" asked Gus.

"You know what happened there," said Hodge, as if it was a surprise to get asked that question. "Toddy thought he could get away with dealing Grant's drugs on a 'one for me, and one for you' basis. Like a child handing out sweets to his best friend in the playground. What a fool. We chased him halfway across Park South, and when we got to Cheney Manor, Grant calmly wandered off for a cup of tea while we laid into him. Grant and Gary were the problems. They enjoyed inflicting pain. For Denver and me, it was just a job. We softened them up, and they did the rest. Grant had an arrangement with that McHugh fellow, the same as you said, and afterwards, they drove away with the body. I helped Denver hose down the sheeting they'd used and tried to get rid of the stench. We heard the truck pull up outside. Gary entered the side door and went to the control panel to operate the roller doors. We ran outside when we heard the noise. Gary spewed his guts when he saw the mess the bullet made of his Dad's head, and when he could stand up straight again, he called Iverson."

"Thank you, Vic," said Gus, "that's been most helpful. Because of your known association with Grant and Gary Burnside, I think you know that a court might find you guilty of the murders you say they committed. You were there throughout each of the instances you described, and it's reasonable to assume you knew what was likely to happen. However, your cooperation will be important, and I'll do what I can to minimise the impact on you when this reaches the courts."

"What do you mean co-operation," said Vic, who suddenly looked puzzled. "I haven't co-operated with anyone. I just told you my side of everything you said you already learned from the others."

"In the long run, you'll agree that it was your best course of action," said Gus. "We're talking to Kerry this afternoon. Is there a message you'd wish us to pass to her?"

Vic Hodge shook his head.

Gus nodded to the warder, and Vic Hodge left the room. The prison officer waited while Gus and Lydia collected their belongings.

"I'll see you out, Mr Freeman, Miss," he said, "did you get everything you wanted?"

"We got far more than I expected," said Gus, "but we're still no closer to identifying Grant Burnside's killer."

"I remember Burnside from my days at HMP Winchester," said the prison officer. "I saw what he did to Manny Franchetti. Grant was a sadistic animal. If it were me, I'd rejoice that Burnside was dead and raise a glass to whoever did the deed. But, I'd never bust a gut to find the person responsible."

"Until we know who did it and why we can't be sure Grant Burnside was their only victim."

"A serial killer who only deals in gang leaders, did you mean?" laughed the prison officer. "Now that's the daftest thing I've heard this week. Time for you to go."

When they were outside the prison and back in the car, Lydia turned to Gus.

"That was sneaky, guv," she said, "Vic Hodge was too thick to realise you tricked him into a confession. I don't think the penny dropped until the very end. Iverson would never have let you get away with that."

"True, but did Vic shout for a lawyer at any point during our meeting?"

"No, he didn't, but...."

"We'll let Gablecross worry about any repercussions. Everything we've uncovered is unrelated to our particular task. They can arrest those responsible and take unsolved cases off the books. I want to hear what Luke and Neil learned from Joseph Burnside first. We still have to talk to Kerry. I want to pursue the niggle that Vic Hodge started when he said that he and Kerry were unhappy with how things went after Grant's death. What things? Are they still going on? We'll forget Andy Wilkinson for now, but we should still visit Fergus McHugh as planned. When we've gathered everything together, we'll present the information to Gablecross. Then we can start with Andy Wilkinson and try to identify our mystery marksman. That's our job, and all this other stuff prevents us from getting on with it."

Gus drove them to Swindon and parked outside Kerry Burnside's building. The layout was much as Gus expected, with the ground floor containing one desk plus a comfortable executive office chair. There were four matching chrome and black leather chairs for clients. A rank of four grey filing cabinets lined the partition wall.

It was basic stuff for a taxi firm Room 101. This was Kerry's domain. The office in which she attempted to convince everyone the Burnsides ran a legitimate business.

Beyond the partition wall were a kitchenette and a cloakroom. Gus couldn't see it from the pavement, but he'd bet his pension on it. Lydia rang the doorbell.

"Kerry must be upstairs in the flat," said Lydia.

"The stairs are right behind the partition wall," said Gus, "with the facilities to your left as you climb to the first floor."

"Have you been here before, guv?" said Lydia.

"No, but I've visited a thousand offices in my career. What more do you need?"

A large woman appeared from where Gus had said the staircase would be. Kerry Burnside matched Jake's description in every respect. She was as tall as Gary and four stones heavier. Nature can be cruel.

"We'll talk in here," said Kerry when she opened the door. When Lydia and Gus eased past her, Kerry flicked the office sign to 'Closed' and made a point of closing the Venetian blinds on each of the windows to prevent passers-by from looking in.

"People around here want to know everyone's business," she said.

Gus explained who they were and why they wished to speak with her this afternoon. Kerry gazed alternately at Gus and then at Lydia. Gus wasn't sure whether she was listening to what he said or sizing them up for a trip to Fergus McHugh.

"How do you get on with the other members of your family, Kerry?" asked Gus.

"I'll stop you there, Mr Freeman," said Kerry, "Patrick's on his way. He won't be a minute. He knows I'm more than capable of answering your questions without embarrassing my brothers, but he's now on his guard, after the stunt you pulled this morning."

"Perhaps it would have helped if you had visited Mr Hodge in Horfield this morning," said Gus, "you could have made sure he said nothing out of turn. Mr Iverson had his hands full in Marlborough, trying to keep Henry and Joseph out of trouble."

Kerry shrugged and allowed herself a brief smile.

"Nice try, Mr Freeman. Patrick warned me about you."

"I can't think why," said Gus, "I only want the truth, and your solicitor agreed to these meetings because he wanted to help the police find your father's killer. We've had nothing but cooperation throughout our conversations so far."

Lydia nudged Gus's arm. If her keen ears weren't deceiving her, Iverson's Jaguar had just pulled up outside. The doorbell rang, and Kerry let him in.

"I hope you haven't asked my client leading questions, Freeman," he said.

Kerry shoved one of the visitor chairs alongside her comfy seat. Iverson placed his briefcase on the desk and sat down.

"Kerry asked us to wait until you joined us," said Gus. "Did Henry and Joseph escape unscathed from this morning's meetings?"

"Of course," said Iverson. "You sent two junior staff members to hide your secret visit to HMP Bristol. I should have known not to trust you, Freeman. You realised that Henry and Joseph could offer you nothing. They're legitimate businessmen who work tirelessly for the family and waste their morning answering stupid questions. Meanwhile, you were interrogating Mr Hodge without the benefit of counsel. I have yet to learn what you think you learned from him, but rest assured, the Burnside family will defend any accusations most strenuously. Vic Hodge is an imbecile. So one must take everything he says with a large pinch of salt."

Lydia watched Kerry Burnside's face. The woman was on the verge of tears.

"I would expect nothing less," said Gus. "My colleague, Ms Logan Barre, recorded our conversation with Mr Hodge. We can provide you with a copy. If you want the names of the prison staff, who were present throughout the meeting, we can also make them available. At no time did Vic Hodge ask for a lawyer to be present. Instead, we told him what we'd learned from our conversations so far, and Vic was kind enough to fill in the odd gap in our knowledge."

"I'll bet," said Iverson.

"Well, what do you expect? Apart from Kerry here, Mr

Hodge felt abandoned by the family. Nobody has spoken to him since he got arrested. Loyalty has to be earned. Can we get to the matter in hand now and start our conversation with Ms Burnside?"

Iverson shrugged. Gus was carrying on, no matter what objections he raised.

Chapter Nine

"WHAT DO YOU WANT TO KNOW?" asked Kerry.

"I'll come to that. But, first, I want you to know that we've spoken to Maggie, Kirstin, Gary, Henry, Joseph, and Vic," said Gus. "Please believe me when I say we didn't leave you until last to upset you. Do you need a moment?"

Lydia knew that Gus hadn't missed Kerry's reaction to Iverson's assessment of Vic Hodge's mental capacity. She produced a tissue from her handbag and stretched across the desk to hand it to her.

Everything stopped while Kerry wiped her eyes and blew her nose.

"The outcome is that I know everything I need about the Sunday morning your father died. Everything except who had the motive and opportunity to kill him. We've made no progress on that front yet."

"I'm not surprised," said Kerry, "my brothers couldn't trace him, either."

"Vic sends his best wishes, by the way," said Gus. "That was a well-kept secret, Kerry. We talked to that long list of

148

people before we visited Vic, and not one mentioned you two in the same breath."

The look on Patrick Iverson's face was priceless.

"It's not what you think," said Kerry. "We aren't together in that way. Maybe we might have something if Vic wasn't in prison and things were different around here. I won't cry myself to sleep every night over it if it doesn't materialise."

"How are things between you and your mother?" asked Gus.

"They've always been fine. But, of course, I don't get to see Mum as much these days because of that little Madam."

"Kirstin, d'you mean?" asked Lydia. "Does she monopolise Maggie's time? Of course, she was with your mother when we interviewed her, but I didn't read too much into that."

"She only married Gary for the money and the prestige," said Kerry. "It's amazing what some women can bear. Kirstin spends a fortune making herself look terrific, wasting it on Gary. He adores his two kids, but he ignores Kirstin most of the time. I've had more meaningful conversations with this desk than those two have had since they got married. I've got no time for her. She distances herself from the business that provides her with the money she squanders."

Gus made a note. Was this another sign that the Burnside fortress had cracks in its defences? According to Gary, differences between family members never existed when they spoke to him yesterday.

"Henry and Joseph are closer to your age, Kerry," said Lydia, "how do you get on with them? They're both single, aren't they? Do you ever socialise together?"

"Their time is precious," sneered Kerry. "Henry and

Joseph never take an hour off from the business. It will drive them into an early grave."

"So, what social life do you have?" asked Lydia.

"Who says I need one?" said Kerry, "I look after the books for the company. I work forty hours a week in this office. My flat upstairs has the luxuries I need. I walk my dogs every night. I don't drink or smoke. Who enjoys going to a cinema or restaurant on their own? My one extravagance is a trip to Horfield prison to visit Vic."

"Didn't you ever go to the snooker club that your Dad and the others used?" asked Gus.

"Are you joking?" said Kerry. "You wouldn't catch me in that hellhole."

"No, I suppose it earned a reputation with the Blake Dixon affair, didn't it?"

"If you check your records, you'll find that the courts cleared Kerry's father of any involvement in that episode, Mr Freeman," said Iverson.

"That club has always had a lousy reputation," said Kerry. "It makes my stomach churn to think of it."

"As the company Chief Financial Officer, you must have rented the warehouse space out at Cheney Manor," said Gus. "Where did you move the operation to after your father's death?"

"Of course, I was involved," said Kerry. "Despite the fancy title that Dad gave me, I manage the financial affairs alone. I do everything. We had a good deal with that Cheney Manor unit, but Gary couldn't face going there again after Dad's death."

"It was understandable. That morning had to bring back unpleasant memories," said Lydia.

"It wasn't just the murder," said Kerry, "Gary prides himself on being a hard man. So he didn't want a constant reminder of his reaction to seeing his father's dead body in the cab."

"Gary was sick, wasn't he," said Gus. "That must have appeared strange to Vic and Denver after the alleged violent altercations they joined in together."

"Careful, Mr Freeman," said Iverson. "Kerry wasn't present that day, and the police have no proof that either man was involved in any of the events you've referred to during these interviews. If Gablecross had any evidence, they would have acted on it."

"Things change, Mr Iverson. I can leave that question for now. I'm more interested to learn about the warehouse space that Kerry rented in June 2014."

Kerry turned to Patrick Iverson.

"You need to leave," she said.

"I'd advise you most strongly that I stay, Kerry. I need to protect the interests of the whole family. Gary wouldn't want me to leave."

Gus and Lydia watched and waited. Neither of them dared say a word.

"Vic's not an imbecile, nor am I," Kerry snapped. "I don't need you sitting on my shoulder like a vulture, checking my every word. You're frightened I might say something that hurts Gary and the precious family. Now get out. I can handle this."

Patrick Iverson collected his briefcase and headed for the front door.

"You're making a big mistake," he said as he slammed the door behind him.

"Do you want a coffee?" asked Kerry. "I reckon things will go easier now that slimy sod has crawled back under his stone."

Well, that was a turn-up for the book, thought Gus.

"I assume I can find everything I need behind the partition wall?" asked Lydia. "You sit and chat with Mr Freeman."

"I could use an office girl," said Kerry. "No matter what you think of the family business, it's tough for one person to manage. Milk and two sugars in mine, thanks."

You could make life easier by not needing two sets of books, Gus thought, but kept it to himself. They were making headway, and he didn't want to stop Kerry now she had opened up.

Lydia returned with three coffees and sat back down next to Gus.

"Have you remembered where you moved your warehousing, Kerry?" asked Gus.

"We rent a unit out at Blagrove, next to the M4," she said, "only five miles from here. It's convenient for Henry and Joseph. The rent costs us twenty per cent more than the old place. But Gary wouldn't listen."

"When you filled in the details in the books," said Gus, "how did you explain payments made to Fergus McHugh? Did your father, or Gary, ever tell you what he did for them?"

"That was the farmer near Blunsdon, wasn't it?" said Kerry. "Dad told me it was waste disposal, and McHugh only dealt in cash. It seemed odd, but there have been plenty of other cash-in-hand transactions I've coped with over the years."

"I've no doubt," said Gus. "Did you ever wonder what type of waste disposal it involved?"

"Dad told me it was nothing I needed to worry over. Sometimes it was best not to know."

"Henry told my detectives this morning that you still

have holiday money belonging to Howard Todd. That seems odd."

"We don't understand where he went," said Kerry. "His sister called in here one day. It wasn't long after Dad's funeral. She told me she believed that her brother was dead. Gary told me Toddy had just left the area. After that, I never had personal dealings with him."

"I can assure you Howard won't be back to collect what's owed him," said Gus.

"Perhaps I should pop the money in an envelope and drop it round to Mandy then," said Kerry, "it's not much, but Gary suggested I held on to it, just in case."

"This will come out in due course, Kerry," said Gus, "but Howard was the reason for your father being at Cheney Manor the day he died. The gunman had nothing to do with Toddy, as your family called him, but at around ten o'clock that morning, he ceased to be one of your employees."

"Vic was there, wasn't he?" asked Kerry.

"Vic's given us useful information, Kerry. I'm inclined to believe him when he says he killed no one. We will take his cooperation into account when the time comes."

"There might be a deal on the table. Is that what you're saying?"

"I can't make that promise, Kerry. It's not my decision. However, my words might carry weight. If you were to cooperate too, it wouldn't hurt his chances of a deal."

"I won't go against my family, Mr Freeman," said Kerry, "but if there's something else I can help you with, I will."

"Do you find it strange that Vic was in prison while Denver Drewett escaped before the police could arrest him?"

"Vic told me they were working together," said Kerry. "Gary sent them to Upper Stratton to have a word with a kid who fell behind with his payments. The boy's mother arrived home out of the blue and saw the company van parked on her driveway. She called the police. Vic got picked up an hour later. The police went to Vic and Denver's homes simultaneously, yet Denver wasn't there. He must have returned home after the job, packed a bag, and legged it."

"Who tipped him off?" asked Lydia.

"There's only one person who would do that," said Kerry.

"Gary?" asked Gus.

Kerry nodded.

"Why, though?" asked Lydia, "those three have been friends since school. If Gary discovered that the police heard of the attack on this person in Upper Stratton, why didn't he warn both of them?"

"Because, and I'm quoting Vic now, Kerry," said Gus, "the longer everything went on after Grant died, the more both of us realised it was wrong."

"Did he tell you anything more about that?" asked Kerry.

"Nothing," said Gus, "would you wish to elaborate?"

Kerry shook her head.

"We'll come back to it later," said Gus, "for now, let's concentrate on things around your father's death. Don't bother denying the facts, Kerry. We're beyond that, and you know it. Your Dad changed the focus of the business from theft to drugs. Grant used Gary, plus his two schoolmates, to persuade people to toe the line, pay up on time, and never say a word about anything they saw or heard. I remember the Gablecross detective's phrase when he spoke with our colleague. It's my way or the highway. Gary followed the same mantra, didn't he? I suppose you keep your distance from street-level business, Kerry. Sleeping at night with that spinning around in your head would be tough. I could tell you were different from Gary when you spoke about the goings-on at the snooker club. You said things such as the Blake Dixon murder made your stomach churn."

"I've tried to keep as far away from it as possible, Mr Freeman," said Kerry, "not the same way as Madam Kirstin, though. She's in total denial. Kirstin has made herself believe that Gary is a genuine businessman. So any talk of violence is just that, talk in her fantasy world."

"Everything ramped up a notch after your Dad died, I imagine?" asked Gus. He was in virgin territory here. These were details that Jake Latimer hadn't passed to Neil.

"Gary ordered Henry to take on a whole load of recruits. Henry had to warn them he'd send Vic and Denver to sort out anyone who didn't follow the methods he laid down. I watched youngsters turn into violent criminals in a matter of months. There was a constant air of casual violence. Henry took on Simeon, a lovely young lad who was only sixteen from the next street. Within weeks he was smashing another kid's head against a brick wall or shoving someone to the ground to build his reputation. You spoke of a phrase that my father used. It's my way or the highway. That's gone now. Henry told his kids that whenever they beat on someone or punished them, they had to say—it's not personal. It's just business."

"Tough to stand by and watch it happen, I imagine?" said Gus.

"The business keeps going from strength to strength," said Kerry, "and things are only getting worse. I came to realise I needed to get out. Sometimes Vic and Denver got the call to assist Gary, and someone got hurt badly. Vic didn't want that. He didn't mind wading into a fight with several blokes his age and size, but he drew the line at beating on children."

"If that got back to Gary, then there's your explanation of why Denver received a tip-off and Vic didn't," said Gus.

"It's such a mess, isn't it?" said Kerry, "Gina could see where it was heading, but nobody took any notice of her."

There it was again, thought Gus. Another name was suddenly popping up that he'd dismissed as irrelevant. He was losing his grip. Neither Jake Latimer nor Jack Sanders considered Gina Burnside anything but a lost cause.

"Do you often speak to your aunt, Kerry?" he asked.

"I haven't seen her in decades, Mr Freeman. She left home as soon as possible but sneaked back to babysit Gary in the early days of Mum and Dad's marriage. Mum was only fifteen when Gary was born; she had Henry at seventeen. Dad wasn't an easy man to live with."

"Maggie told us about the abuse, Kerry. I imagine sometimes her injuries meant she couldn't cope with baby Henry and the toddler, Gary,"

"Gary was eight when I came along. Mum was pregnant with me when Dad went to prison at the end of 1977. He was away for four years. That was when Auntie Gina spent the most time with Mum and us kids."

"What did Gina see in Gary's behaviour that made her think trouble lay ahead?"

"Gary had a problem with confined spaces," said Kerry. "When he was a toddler, Gina said she'd put him in his cot after his feed, and he'd settle for a while. Can you remember what you were like at that age?"

Gus couldn't remember a thing from that far back.

"Just about," said Lydia, "I was afraid of the dark, and

my parents left a light on at the top of the stairs, outside my room, so when I awoke, it wasn't pitch black."

"Yeah, me too," said Kerry. "But Gary moved around in his cot and burrowed under the blanket. His head was at the foot, and his feet stuck out at the top. So he couldn't get out when he woke up and screamed the house down. Gina ran into the bedroom the first time it happened and comforted him. She said Gary's face was as red as a beetroot, and he looked so angry. So when she told Mum, they made sure his bedclothes were always loose so that he could escape."

"Was that it?" asked Gus, "I would have thought Gary grew out of that as soon as he moved into a bed. But, surely, you two weren't still afraid of the dark after you reached school age or a little later?"

Kerry and Lydia didn't reply. Gus knew better than to press them for an answer.

"Do you know what many kids say was their favourite toy growing up?" asked Kerry, "not a doll or a train set. A cardboard box. Something to climb in and out of and play to your heart's content. That box became anything your imagination could dream of, a fairy coach or a spaceship, but for Gary, it was different. Henry and Joseph played together in a large box containing a Christmas present Mum and Dad bought for Gary. He didn't like seeing Henry and Joseph enjoying themselves. So Gary tipped the box over and made them get out. It's my box, he yelled and climbed inside. Henry closed the lid, and then he and Joseph sat on top, trapping Gary inside."

"I think I can guess what happened," said Gus, "Gary lost his temper."

"When they stood up, Gary burst out of that box like the Incredible Hulk. I was on Mum's knee, and she was reading me a story. I was three at the time, but I remember it vividly. Gary attacked Henry and Joseph with his fists and his feet. By the time Mum plopped me in the chair and went to drag him away, they both had bloody noses and split lips. Henry's little finger got broken too. Gary was a madman."

"So, Gina spotted his aggressive nature from infancy," said Gus, "and confined spaces were a trigger."

"Yet, Gary still chose a life of crime and the potential for getting locked up in a cell," said Lydia. "I would have thought it was the last thing he wanted."

"Gary didn't choose his way of life," said Kerry, "none of my brothers did. Instead, our father set them on the same road his father forced him to follow. Grandfather George wanted his legacy to be a Burnside dynasty, where every child followed in his footsteps."

"Why did your Aunt Gina leave home at sixteen?" asked Gus.

"Nobody has ever spoken about it," said Kerry. "When Dad came out of prison and saw me for the first time, Mum said he burst into tears. She never told me that until I was twelve. I thought he wanted another son. She shook her head and said that when his father died in 1988, a weight lifted off his shoulders. I didn't understand what she meant, and Mum's never mentioned it since. It seems to be a Burnside way. Any family secrets get buried deep."

Gus and Lydia drew their own conclusions.

"Where would we find Gina?" asked Gus.

"I don't know her address," said Kerry, "she keeps moving."

"We'll find her if we need to speak with her," said Gus. "I appreciate how difficult this afternoon has been for you, Kerry. I hope we haven't caused you too much distress."

"What will happen now?" asked Kerry.

"I say the same thing to each person we interview on this case," said Gus. "The entire purpose of the Crime Review Team is to find answers to a case that detectives left unsolved. I do not understand who killed your father or why. As for any conclusions one can discern from the interviews we've held, that's for detectives at Gablecross to determine and act upon. Those matters don't come within our purview. So we'll let you get on with your day. If you feel ready to add to what you shared with us today, I suggest you speak to someone at Gablecross. Tell them the full story. If you have information about your father's murder, that's the only thing that would necessitate us meeting again."

"You'll inform Swindon police of what Vic and I have told you, though, won't you?" asked Kerry.

"We keep them informed of everything we uncover, Kerry," said Gus. "They would have highlighted your father's murder when our superiors at Devizes asked for cases that deserved a second look. They're as keen as we are to bring his killer to justice finally. I just wish we could find a starting point."

Gus and Lydia left Kerry Burnside worrying over her uncertain future.

"Who do we talk to next, guv?" asked Lydia.

"I think we've done enough for today. I want to return to the office, listen to what Luke and Neil learned from Joseph, if anything, and then prepare for tomorrow."

"Did you imagine that Gary Burnside could be so volatile when you interviewed him, guv?"

"He had his minder with him," said Gus. "Iverson would recognise the signs and cut off any line of questioning that might cause Gary to explode. Perhaps Grant had the same trait. Grant and Gary killed at least three men while working together. Vic's claim that they played no part in the killings looks more credible after our conversation with Kerry. However, it doesn't get him off the hook for other things he did for the Burnside family."

Gus drove them back to the Old Police Station office, and they soon reunited with Neil Davis and Luke Sherman. One look at the Freeman Files told Gus what he needed to know. Luke and Neil's reports on their interviews with Henry and Joseph were a carbon copy of one another.

"Was Joseph listening in to Henry's answers to your questions?" he asked, tongue in cheek.

"He wasn't," said Luke, "but I don't believe they rehearsed their responses. We didn't learn an awful lot, I'm afraid. Was my text message of any use?"

"Gus found a way to use it to our advantage," said Lydia, with a grin at her boss.

"That message was timely, Neil," said Gus, "and let's leave it at that."

"I hope you fared better at HMP Bristol and with Kerry Burnside, guv," said Neil, "because otherwise, today's been a waste of effort."

Gus gave the pair the headlines from their interviews with Vic Hodges and Kerry.

Lydia continued entering her reports into the files and listened to their reactions.

"Kerry and Vic Hodges," said Neil. "Wait until I tell Jake Latimer. He won't believe it. I'm not surprised he missed it, mind. Gablecross would have eyes on drug trafficking and dealing, trying to catch a break. Vic's been inside for a while, and where Kerry might go on a Wednesday afternoon isn't important enough for someone to tail her."

"I bet you didn't know where to look when she

dismissed her brief, guv," said Luke, "does she stand a chance of escaping the gang's clutches, do you think?"

"Gablecross would demand more from Kerry than she divulged to us before any deal could be on the table," said Gus. "She was holding something back."

"But if they considered Vic and Kerry as a couple," said Lydia, "then the combination of their evidence could bring the whole Burnside gang crashing down. Then they could weigh the value of that evidence against the crimes they both committed. It might lead to a reduction in any sentences they had to serve."

"There's a long way to go before Gablecross will get to that," said Gus. "I'll enter my notes and impressions into the Freeman Files now. We're almost ready to pass our findings on to Gablecross. Tomorrow morning, I'm taking a trip to Swindon to find Gina Burnside. I want to learn more about her and her assessment of Gary."

"Take care driving around Broadgreen, guv," said Neil, "I'd hate to hear a zealous beat officer cautioned you for kerb-crawling."

"Fat chance of finding one, Neil," said Gus, "so. I think I'll risk it."

"What do you want us to do in the morning, guv?" asked Luke.

"I'll go to Broadgreen direct from Urchfont. If you collect Neil on the way to Swindon from your place in Warminster, I'd like you to do two things for me. First, check out Andy Wilkinson and grill him on Grant Burnside's day of reckoning. Second, see if he spotted anyone hanging around the site the week before. You know the question we need to ask. After that, Neil, could you liaise with Jake Latimer? Find a young tearaway called Simeon. I didn't get a surname, but he lived within a stone's throw of

Kerry's office, and Henry's had him on his books for a while."

"How old is this lad, guv?" asked Neil.

"Maybe seventeen or eighteen, Neil," said Gus.

"I'm holding the fort then, guv," said Lydia.

"Who better?" said Gus. "You can spend the morning checking the office layout I sketched on that board over there. Then, if we don't make it back from Swindon before the furniture arrives, make sure it goes where it should. Keep the crew supplied with coffee and biscuits, flutter your eyelashes, but don't let them leave until there's nothing for us to do when we get back."

"Got it, guv," said Lydia, "but you'll be back by then, surely? Ladies in Gina Burnside's profession don't want customers stopping them from working for an entire morning."

Gus was already updating his file and missed the looks his team shared while he concentrated on his keyboard. Instead, he heard the stifled laughter and wondered what he would do with the information Gina Burnside might offer.

At five o'clock, the members of the Crime Review Team finished work and headed home. As Gus exited the lift on the ground floor, he stood to watch the three cars leaving the car park ahead of him.

Yes, they were a good bunch. Everyone put in a decent shift today, yet Gus knew that his team still had nothing tangible to show for it.

Ah, well, tomorrow was another day.

Chapter Ten

Friday, 22 June 2018

GUS SPENT Thursday evening deep in thought. There was no visit from Suzie Ferris tonight to look forward to, and he knew that the weekend was time enough to get more gardening done. Clemency Bentham and Bert Penman had to labour on without his company.

Tonight was one of those nights where he needed to be alone to mull over this case that was causing them so many problems. Gus couldn't waste time hunting for something to eat, let alone cook it, so he dialled a familiar number. His pizza would arrive in thirty minutes.

He walked through to the lounge to select the right music to accompany his musings. He toyed with a Pink Floyd album but cast it aside after seeing Joyce Pemberton Smythe's framed letter.

Was there something with a French influence in his collection? Cajun Renaissance with the Lost Bayou

Ramblers might fit the bill. He turned up the volume, poured a glass of Malbec and let his mind wander.

Sometimes, things work out the way you plan. You go through each stage other times, checking every likely response a suspect or witness might give. Then, something happens that throws everything up in the air.

Gus reached Swindon at ten o'clock. He started the search for Gina Burnside. By twelve, he felt like a kid on the beach who spent hours constructing the perfect sandcastle when somebody ran past, sending sand flying high into the air.

It started with a phone call.

"Jake Latimer," asked Gus, "Gus Freeman, here. Can you tell me where to find Gina Burnside at this time of day?"

"Gina is rarely on the streets in the mornings, guv," said Jake, "the light's too harsh. At sixty-three, Gina relies on her punters not seeing too well under the dim street lights on dark corners. I can tell you where she might have gone for a pick-me-up, though. That's a euphemism for a fix. Gina started using years ago, and she's not a pretty sight. So what are you after, anyway?"

"Knowledge, Jake," said Gus, "where's this address?"

Jake told Gus the best place to start on his search for Gina. Gus headed into Broadgreen and sought out Gladstone Street. He drove up and down twice before he spotted her. There was no mistaking that she was Grant's sister. He pulled up ahead of Gina and wound down the passenger-side window. He prayed it would wind up again once she'd left.

"Gina," he called as she passed him. Gina stopped and turned back. Her straggly blonde hair should have been white by now, but needs must when the needle drives. Her emaciated features told their own story. Gina leaned in the open window.

"Yes, dear, are you looking for something special?"

"Why don't you get in the car?" said Gus. "We don't want the neighbours calling the police, do we?"

Gina opened the passenger door and slid into the seat beside him. Gus thought Jake was right. She was wearing a skirt that was way too short for a woman her age. But, with the warm summer sun encouraging Gus to wear a short-sleeved shirt today, Gina persisted in tugging at the sleeves of her long-sleeved cardigan. She wanted to hide her painfully thin arms and the tracks marking her as an addict.

"It's a fiver for the hand and a tenner for a blow," said Gina, "drive around the corner. I know a quiet spot, dear."

"I only want to talk, Gina," said Gus,

"Talk?" said Gina, "that'll be twenty quid then. I don't want to hear about your crap life. I've got enough troubles of my own."

"Look, Gina, I'll gladly give you twenty quid, provided you promise to spend it on food and not drink or drugs. My name's Freeman, by the way, a consultant with Wiltshire Police."

Gina moved her hand towards the door. Gus moved off from the kerb and drove around Broadgreen.

"Don't try anything stupid, Gina. I want to ask you about Gary, your nephew."

"He's a wrong 'un," said Gina. "I told Maggie, but she wouldn't go against my brother. Grant hit her often enough as it was without her telling Grant his kid was a sadist."

"Kerry told me yesterday that you first noticed something when you babysat for Maggie."

"You spoke to Kerry?" asked Gina.

"We're speaking to everyone in the family. That's why I came to see you."

"You won't get any sense out of our Glyn. He's lost his marbles, poor beggar,"

"We needn't bother Glyn, don't worry. However, Gary has a violent temper, hasn't he, Gina, and confined spaces can trigger it."

"At the start, they did, yeah, but the other trouble started when he went to prison."

"What do you mean by the other trouble, Gina?" asked Gus.

"Grant warned his sons to stay tough and show the others you were a hard man if they went inside. He said that if you showed any sign of weakness, they'd be on you. The cells were big enough for Gary to control his fears, but the bars on the windows played on his mind. Several of the real hard men started picking on him. You can guess the rest."

"Gary suffered abuse," said Gus.

"Two of them pinned him down while the other inmate raped him. They took it in turns. Gary told his Dad he stared at those bars through every second of his ordeal and swore it would never happen again. Of course, it didn't, but it changed something inside his head. He was never the same after that."

"He hasn't spent any time in prison since that stretch, has he?" asked Gus.

"If you can't swim, keep away from water," said Gina. "Yet, Gary keeps going to that snooker club. He can't resist it. As I said, he changed after what happened. He's paid those inmates back ten times over."

Gus wasn't sure what Gina was telling him. Was Gary

an abuser? Yesterday Kerry gave a hint that George Burnside had had a dark side.

"Why did you leave home at sixteen, Gina?" he asked.

"I don't want to talk about that. Where's my twenty quid? I want you to stop the car now."

"Your father abused you, didn't he? How old were you when that started? Twelve? Thirteen? That's why Grant was so upset when Kerry was born. He feared that his father would rape her, too, in time. Kerry was ten when George died, and Maggie told Kerry that it was as if a weight had lifted off Grant's shoulders but never explained why."

"What could I do?" sobbed Gina. "Nobody would believe me. I walked away as soon as I reached sixteen. He ruined me. I left school with no qualifications, and I felt worthless. All I could do was accept I'd never amount to anything and sell the only thing I had that men wanted. After two years in that game, I realised I could never make a decent life with a man. Any good years I had are behind me now. I barely scrape a living, and most of the money I make goes in my arm."

"There are people who can help you, Gina," said Gus.

Only a few weeks ago, he and his team had visited this area of Swindon to look into Laura Mallinder's murder. Theo Hickerton and Jake Latimer had made a point of stressing the excellent work carried out by the local Outreach Project. The area's reputation had improved back in 2011 when Laura died, but sex workers had returned in more significant numbers once more.

"I've seen the van," said Gina, "the younger girls tell me to go, but what's the point?"

"The project offers practical and emotional support to women involved in street-based sex working, Gina," said Gus. "Wiltshire Police supplies a simple, unmarked van, and members of my team have seen it in action. The van parks in the same spot on Manchester Road every week, stocked with food donated by a local bakery. It's not just free food and a hot drink. There are clothes that people have donated and a friendly chat on offer. All of you are vulnerable. We've seen the number of attacks on sex workers escalate in the past two years. You're not alone, Gina. Few of you choose the life you lead, and you need help to get off the drugs you just bought. So why not think about it?"

Gus handed Gina two twenty-pound notes.

"Remember what I said. Use it wisely."

"Bless you, dear. I've tried to quit," sobbed Gina, "I have, honest. But getting high, even if it's only an hour or two, helps get me through another day doing what I must do. So stop the car, Mr Freeman. Here's the squat where I'm staying for now. I know you mean well, but I'm beyond help."

Gus let her go. What more could he do? He watched Gina knock on the door of the boarded-up house, and someone let her inside. At least she had a roof over her head. He drove away from Broadgreen and headed to where Neil told him he would find the snooker club.

The building looked deserted. Gus didn't know what time a club such as this opened. He parked outside and tried the door. It was locked. A faded notice in a glass-fronted wooden cabinet on the wall to the left of the door informed him that the club opened from noon until midnight.

According to another notice, six snooker tables and six 8-Ball pool tables were available. Dress must be smart casual, and strict conditions applied regarding behaviour on the tables and in the social areas. Gus couldn't see that anyone had a problem with that. Yet Kerry called the club a hellhole, and Gina didn't have a kind word. So what was the truth?

He checked his watch—only a few minutes to twelve. Gus returned to his car and tried to close the passenger-side window. He should have known it wouldn't play ball. As another vehicle arrived behind him and parked, he persuaded the window to close. His day was getting better. The club manager had his keys in his hand and was opening the doors.

"Good morning," said Gus, "I'm not desperate to play on one of your tables, but I am keen to see inside."

"If you're looking to buy the place, make me an offer," said the younger man. "My name's Asif. These clubs aren't as popular as they were. I've no idea why. Since Hearn took over World Snooker, there's been lashings of money in the game. Every sixteen-year-old boy and girl in the UK with a talent for potting a ball should stand outside this door with a cue waiting for me to open up. Five hours of practice and coaching every day and the world's your oyster. Who needs to slog your guts out at Honda or stack shelves in Tesco? There are tournaments every week of the year. Why not travel the world and play a game that's never affected by the weather?"

Gus hadn't realised there was that much money available.

"I'm not looking to buy, I'm afraid, Asif," said Gus, "My name is Freeman, a consultant with Wiltshire Police. However, a person of interest comes here regularly, Gary Burnside. Do you expect to see him today?"

Asif stopped in the foyer.

"I wouldn't feel able to say this to anyone else, Mr Freeman, but if you work with the police, then I'll risk it. If I could stop that man from coming here, I would. His money keeps this club afloat, but he's a menace."

"Have you been manager here long?" Gus asked.

"Two years," said Asif, "my uncle ran the club before me. He was here when that guy got shot."

"Blake Dixon? Yes, I know about that. Grant and Gary Burnside were here that night. Somehow they literally got away with murder."

"Gary was here last night when I left," said Asif. "He booked the Matchroom again."

"Didn't you have to see him off the premises at midnight?"

"Have you met Gary Burnside, Mr Freeman? You don't tell him to leave. I've left him in there frequently. Gary slams the door behind him on the way out. It's a standard Yale lock. There's not much here worth stealing once we bring the shutters to ground level around the social area. There are days when I hope that the youngsters around here burn the place to the ground. It might be the only way to get out without losing a fortune."

Asif led Gus to the bar area, and he started unlocking the steel shutters.

"If you go straight through the door ahead of you, you'll see the Matchroom on your left. We cover the other snooker and pool tables over until the punters arrive. I doubt anyone will drift in here until late afternoon. When they finish work on a Friday, most people want to head for a noisy bar, not a club, for a quiet game of snooker or pool."

Gus opened the door to the games room. The smell hit him straight away.

"Phone for the police, Asif," he called. "You've had a break-in through the fire door on the far side, and I don't like the smell of what's behind the Matchroom door."

"What the heck has that animal Burnside done now?" said Asif, getting his mobile phone out of his pocket. Two uniformed officers arrived within ten minutes.

"What's going on, Asif?" said one of the young officers.

"Mr Freeman and I came inside at noon. First, we chatted in here, and then he wanted to check out the Matchroom."

"Who are you, then?" asked the other young policeman.

Gus showed him his identification.

"My Crime Review Team is taking a fresh look at Grant Burnside's murder in 2014," said Gus, "you were still at school when that happened. Since we started our investigations, we've been in constant touch with DS Jake Latimer at your station, so it might be a good idea to give him a head's up. Asif and I have touched nothing beyond this inner door. This morning, I aimed to understand more about Grant's son, Gary Burnside. We interviewed Gary earlier in the week, and following conversations with other relatives of his, I wanted to familiarise myself with the layout of this club and what happens here."

"What do you reckon is behind that door?"

"What's your name, son?" asked Gus.

"PCSO Travers, Sir,"

"You need only call me Mr Freeman," said Gus. "When you've found as many dead bodies as I have, Travers, you'll recognise the smell. We need a full team in here in due course, but I'll fetch my blue paper suit from the boot of my car and gloves for the time being. If you're happy, I'll take a quick look. You get on with contacting DS Latimer. He'll do the necessary."

The uniformed officer and the Community Support Officer nodded meekly. This wasn't a simple break-in and a blocked toilet.

Gus returned two minutes later dressed, ready for the fray.

"That's where they came in after midnight last night," he said, pointing to the fire door.

Gus saw the puzzled faces staring at him.

"Look at where the doors are damaged. Someone used a crowbar outside to gain access. It wasn't someone trying to get out. You only need to smack the exit handle. You know what a big unit Gary Burnside is. One bloke would not tackle him alone. As for why it had to be after midnight?"

"That's when I left," Asif told them.

"Oh, right," said Travers.

"The public is in safe hands, Asif," said Gus as he walked towards the Matchroom door.

Gary Burnside lay face up on the snooker table.

Blood saturated the green baize cloth.

Gus stood in the doorway, studying the rest of the room.

Behind him, Gus heard retching.

"Travers? If that's you, get outside before contaminating the crime scene."

Gus heard someone run for the door.

Gus recapped his first impressions. Gary Burnside died in a frenzied attack involving several assailants. What was going on in here when those assailants arrived? Burnside's designer jeans and underwear were around his knees. Gus moved closer.

Ye Gods! He could see the butt of a snooker cue. Gus checked the racks at the side of the room. A broken cue lay discarded on the floor next to the stand containing various cues and rests.

Gus wondered whether someone had shoved the butt into Gary's body before or after he died. It had to be significant. The information he'd gathered from Kerry and Gina was falling into place.

The back wall provided the last piece of the jigsaw. Its narrow windows, perhaps a foot from the ceiling, had steel bars to deter intruders. The windows could open outward using a winding mechanism attached to the left-hand wall. Gus could imagine this room was Gary's worst nightmare.

Gus could hear other people entering the club behind him. The cavalry had arrived.

"By the centre, Gus, what's been happening here? Is that Gary Burnside?"

"Good afternoon, Jake, and well-spotted," said Gus. "Who's SIO on this case?"

"Someone you know, Gus. DI Francis moved here from Devizes last week. For some reason, your ACC thought his talents were needed elsewhere."

Gus sighed. Gareth Francis wasn't a lousy copper, but he could be dense. Geoff Mercer and Suzie Ferris thought Gus gave him an unwarranted hard time whenever their paths crossed. Kenneth Truelove was wasting no time ridding London Road of deadwood.

"Hello, hello," said Gareth Francis, "what are you doing here, Freeman?"

"I found the body, Gareth," said Gus.

Gareth stood beside Gus, suited and booted, in the appropriate manner. He was off to a good start, at least.

"Forced entry, side door," said Gus.

"I beg your pardon?" said Gareth, inspecting Gary Burnside's body.

"Not in here. Out there, in the games room."

Gareth swallowed hard and managed to hold onto his early lunch.

"This has the signs of being a gangland killing," said

Gareth, "we'd better round up the usual suspects. Which mob do you think was responsible? Bristol, Reading, or a London gang looking for fresh fields? What made you want to call in here, anyway? Do you play?"

"I don't," said Gus, "but I've watched the occasional game on TV. I walked around the table just before you arrived, and I'm afraid the black ball is missing."

"Game over," said Gareth.

"Quite," said Gus, "I think you should carry on with things now, as you are SIO. I'm not supposed to get involved with live cases. A word in your ear, Gareth, before I go."

Gareth Francis and Gus Freeman walked out of the Matchroom and returned to the bar area. Gus told him about his meeting that morning with Gina Burnside.

"Gary Burnside got attacked while in prison in 1997. Two men held him while another inmate raped him. The other two then took their turn. Gary told Grant Burnside that he stared at the bars on the cell windows throughout and swore it would never happen again. Gina told me it changed something inside Gary's head, and he was never the same. Grant wanted his boys to be as hard as him, but I've seen Henry and Joseph. They're not fighters. Gary had the build, but he was a bully rather than a natural thug. He used Denver Drewett and Vic Hodge to carry out the soft-ening-up process. Gary could only function when his victims were out on their feet."

"I'm not sure I follow," said Gareth, "what happened last night?"

"The same thing crops up during the interviews we've had this week. Gary was the one who used this place regularly. Especially after his jail term. My guess is you won't find a gangland connection. You need to speak with Asif, the manager, and perhaps his uncle, who ran the club when Blake Dixon died here."

DI Francis was making notes of everything Gus suggested. Gus smiled to himself.

"What you're looking for are the names of young lads who have been members of this club," said Gus. "I doubt if they still come here. Concentrate on those fourteen to sixteen at the time they joined. Asif told me this club is nowhere near as busy as it was several years ago, so you might only check on thirty or forty young men."

"How many young men do you think were here last night?" asked Gareth.

"I can't do all the work for you, Gareth," said Gus, "I'm supposed to be finding Grant Burnside's killer, not Gary's. I'll tell you what, have a chat with Geoff Mercer at the weekend. Get him to lean on the Acting Chief Constable to see whether they'll release me from my straitjacket. I think I know who killed Gary, but there's work for forensics and the Police Surgeon to do before I can be sure. Is this the first murder for you as Senior Investigation Officer?"

"Is it that obvious?" asked Gareth.

"We all had to start somewhere. The Police Surgeon will tell you to wait until he's completed his long list of tasks but ask him to let you see the black ball as soon as possible."

"I'm not sure I want to," said Gareth with a shudder.

"After he's removed it, Gareth."

"Oh, right. Got it."

Gus took one last look around the snooker club. Asif saw him and wandered over.

"I've locked up for the afternoon," he said, "we won't make any money, anyway."

"Look on the bright side, Asif," said Gus, "the Burnside gang won't be using this place anymore. Members that

Grant and Gary scared off might return as soon as they hear the news."

"I was looking at the plans while you were in there with those detectives," said Asif. "If I have the interior walls removed, get rid of the Matchroom altogether, I can fit in two 9-ball American pool tables."

"That's the spirit," said Gus.

"Will you come back to see how it looks?" asked Asif.

"Don't take this the wrong way," said Gus. "As if."

"If you change your mind, you know," the younger man said.

The wide grin told Gus that Asif forgave him. Perhaps he would call back one day.

Gus drove back towards Devizes, wondering if he should call into London Road to report their progress this week to the ACC. However, on balance, he decided he should let Gareth Francis argue his case for Gus's help rather than forewarn him that he would get a call.

He arrived at the Old Police Station to find it was a hive of activity. The office furniture had arrived. The CRT car park contained three cars and a large van. There didn't appear to be any vacant spaces in the remainder of the municipal car park. Gus drove back out and headed for the main street. He wasn't a great lover of the Crown, but they did a good cup of coffee. He called Neil Davis.

"Neil," said Gus, "are you and Luke free to talk?"

"It's a madhouse up here, guv. I don't think the speaker-phone is the answer."

"Apologise to Lydia. Get yourselves to the Crown. I'll only be in the way up there. Lydia will cope. We needn't waste the afternoon. I have news for you."

Neil and Luke joined him in the bar.

"I ordered coffee for you two," said Gus. "We're all driving later."

"No worries, guv," said Neil, "what news did you bring us?"

"Someone murdered Gary Burnside last night," said Gus.

"Blimey," said Neil. "I thought you were in Broadgreen chatting with Gina. When did you learn about Gary?"

"I found the body in the snooker club," said Gus and updated them on the morning events.

"I think I'm following your thought processes now, guv," said Luke. "You reckon that instead of looking for revenge against the men who raped him, Gary switched his anger to young lads who frequented the snooker club. The Match-room is significant in that respect. Gary flashed his money around in the club, booking the private room night after night. He was the best player there, so he approached a victim, told him he showed the potential to be a top player and took him into the Matchroom for one-to-one coaching. Of course, the settings are different, but in prison, Gary got pinned down with his head forced into the bedding, staring at the barred windows. Gary could show his dominance in the Matchroom as his victims stared at the bars above them."

"Burnside was one sick puppy," said Neil.

"DI Francis will have his work cut out, reducing the number of junior club members to identify those Gary abused," said Luke. "Many of them will be too ashamed to admit it."

"True," said Gus, "but Gareth should try his best. Those lads deserve nothing less."

"Why has nobody ever come forward?" asked Luke.

"That's easy," said Neil, "everyone in Swindon knows

you don't go up against a Burnside. One word out of line, and you're for the high jump."

"Or the pig farm," said Luke.

"So, Gary attacked these kids and threatened them, and possibly their families, with what would happen if they ever breathed a word."

"Burnside strutted about in that club as if he owned the place. It's easy to imagine the previous owner letting Gary know the names and details of any kids he favoured."

"I know where you live, you mean?" said Neil. "Yeah, that sounds right. What a swine."

The three men sat quietly, drinking their coffees.

"We're missing something," said Neil, "The boss has that look in his eye."

"It will keep until Monday," said Gus, "we're hunting another killer. Tell me about young Simeon and Andy Wilkinson."

"It's Simeon Young, guv," said Neil, "and he's eighteen and a half. He did work for Henry, but he's out of the game now. Simeon's working for that engineer bloke who revolutionised the vacuum cleaner. When he was growing up, Simeon told us that his best friend, Frankie, died after getting stabbed. Frankie was thirteen. And Simeon realised what the world was about for people like him, and he started carrying a knife for protection. One day, in Pinehurst, Simeon got into a scuffle on the streets, and these lads wanted to escalate the situation. He could only remember falling to the ground. One of them stabbed him. Simeon said he couldn't believe it when his entire life flashed before his eyes. He was lying on the ground, and a girl held his hand. Simeon thought of the things he still wanted to achieve, like becoming a professional footballer. Instead of sticking at that, he'd thought it better to hang out with his mates selling drugs on the streets for Henry Burnside. Now, look where it got him, he thought. An ambulance arrived and took him to the hospital, and the doctors told Simeon he would not die. It hurt like hell, and it was a hard road before he could play football again. Simeon changed his life after he came out of that hospital. He realised the knife he carried didn't protect him, and it didn't make him a better person. That's when he stopped taking a knife when he went out. If you did, he said, you were more likely to get injured or murdered. He was more likely to end up in jail. Simeon understood that now. It took eleven stitches in his side to make him wake up.

"I asked him what happened to the girl who held his hand," said Luke.

"Simeon told us he never saw her again," said Neil, "she was the girlfriend of the guy who stabbed him. Funny old world, isn't it, guv?"

"Tugs at the heartstrings, doesn't it?" said Gus, "Let's hope someone at Gablecross can utilise that to motivate a few dozen more kids to follow in Simeon's footsteps. Knife crime is out of control. I wondered whether that lad might prove more useful. Maybe Kerry took a shine to him. Never mind, let's move on to Cheney Manor Industrial Estate."

"We found Andy Wilkinson tinkering with an Alfa Romeo guv," said Luke.

"You can forget about taking your Ford Focus to him for a health check," said Neil. "Our Andy's moved up in the world in the past four years. Classic motors only."

Gus would claim that his Focus *was* a classic, but then he remembered the window problem he'd had this morning.

"Moving on," he muttered, "what did he tell you about the morning Grant Burnside died?"

"Wilkinson remembered it alright, guv," said Neil, "It's

been the only bit of excitement since he's worked there. He arrived on the dot of nine that morning and started work on the Saab. Andy told the police he was underneath the car when the Burnsides arrived. We pressed him on that because he seemed edgy."

"He admitted that he watched them leaving, guv. He was taking a break and pouring a cuppa from his flask. Grant and his son were in the van. Wilkinson watched them turn onto the road that leads to McHugh's farm. Then, as he finished his drink, Wilkinson glanced towards the back of the lot. The roller doors were open, and he saw two men inside. But, unfortunately, he couldn't identify them from that distance."

"All he's doing is confirming what we already knew," said Gus. "I don't care if he waved at the Mercedes when it passed his place on the way back. Did he see the gunman?"

"Wilkinson didn't see a soul near his row of buildings that morning, guv," said Luke, "he was adamant about that. He said that he'd remember if he'd seen a bloke dressed in camouflage gear with a rifle and telescopic sight."

"Damn it," said Gus, "another dead end."

"He saw a minivan with a logo on the side two weeks earlier, guv," said Neil. "It drove around the site for twenty minutes and left without stopping."

"Did he get a registration?" asked Gus.

Neil shook his head. "He clocked the driver, though. A rugged-looking bloke in his thirties with ginger hair."

"Any idea of the company he represented? What type of logo was it?"

"It's been four years, guv," said Luke. "Wilkinson didn't remember any specifics. However, the red-haired man made a second appearance on the Friday afternoon before the murder."

"At last, we're getting somewhere," said Gus.

"Andy had driven a car out of his unit to park it ready for the client to collect," said Neil. "He saw someone at the far end of his row of units looking up at the roof. When the bloke spotted Andy looking at him, he disappeared around the end of the building."

"That's the end with the steel ladder he used to climb onto the roof," said Gus, "and where he lay in wait for Grant Burnside on Sunday morning. If only we had CCTV images to look at."

"That's not the sticking point for me," said Luke. "Okay, we triggered a memory of the gunman, but how did the red-haired man know where to be and when? I can't get my head around that."

Gus had to agree. That was a project for next week.

Chapter Eleven

Saturday, 23 June 2018

SUZIE HAD ARRIVED YESTERDAY EVENING, and they had eaten at home, talked through their working week, and fallen asleep in each other's arms after making love. When Suzie disappeared to Worton for her morning ride, Gus started on his long list of chores. First, he pottered in the bungalow's garden and raked the driveway gravel for the umpteenth time. Then, after an hour, he strolled along the lane to the allotment.

Gus waved to several familiar faces on the far side of the field, but his neighbours, Bert Penman and Clemency Bentham were not around. He had the quiet he needed to mull over the events of the past five days. When Suzie joined him at two o'clock, it surprised her how much he'd achieved.

"Did you not stop for lunch?" Suzie asked. Gus shook his head.

"I worked steadily on those things I'd left far too long,"

he said. "Because I got lost in this blessed case of ours, I didn't give time, or food, a thought."

Suzie offered to prepare lunch and returned to the bungalow. Gus worked for another thirty minutes, closed up his shed, and walked home.

"You missed a call," she said as he kicked off his gardening shoes on the step outside the front door.

"Who from?" he replied, hoping it was good news from Kenneth Truelove.

"Patrick Iverson. I noted his number for you."

Gus groaned.

"I had better call back."

Gus stood in the hallway in his socks and dialled.

"Iverson here,"

"You wanted to speak with me," said Gus.

"A nasty business, Mr Freeman," said Iverson.

"Are you referring to what the Burnside family is engaged in or your senior client's murder?"

"Freeman, I know you don't like me, nor the family I represent, but I got trapped like many others that fell into the Burnsides' clutches. Their employees find it difficult to walk away, as you have learned. So I got in touch with Kerry later on Thursday to mend fences. Kerry told me her plans and how much she had shared with you."

"How does this relate to what I discovered yesterday at the snooker club?"

"Kerry gave you an insight into Gary's marriage to Kirstin. She mentioned that you might have spoken with Gina."

"I visited Gina yesterday morning," said Gus, "I know what happened when Gary was in prison. He wasn't brave enough to tackle the men who attacked him, so he assaulted many teenage boys at the snooker club. Then, finally, someone found the nerve to fight back."

"You understand part of what happened, Mr Freeman," said Iverson. "Did you ever wonder about the timing of the attack on Gary?"

"Go on," said Gus, "I'm listening."

"Grant attacked Manny Franchetti in Winchester prison in 1997. Gary's spell inside began early the following year. Everyone was watching Grant and Manny for the Reading gangster to take his revenge. Franchetti sent word to his gang members on the outside to call in a few favours. The three men who attacked Gary belonged to three separate gangs in Bristol, Cardiff, and Birmingham. The authorities never made the connection."

"That explains why the attacks happened," said Gus, "but why did Gary respond in the way he did?"

"Gary was a bully and a coward," said Iverson, "who had urges to hide from his father. There was no way Grant Burnside would ever accept Gary coming out. So, Gary buried his true feelings, married a beautiful woman, had a family, and acted tough whenever needed. Unfortunately, those prison rapes led to violent outbursts, resulting in at least twelve men getting killed, including Spencer Curtis, Blake Dixon, and Howard Todd."

"You don't have to defend them anymore, do you?" said Gus. "Grant and Gary were killers in tandem. While Hodge and Drewett only battered people and cleared up their employers' mess. Grant and Gary are both dead. I suppose the remaining family members won't object to you standing aside. Your life is no longer in danger."

"I hope you're right. As you say, Henry, Joseph, and Kerry are not violent. They will need a talented lawyer when the time comes. Perhaps they will keep my services until that's over. When it is, it will be time for me to retire. I never knew what sort of man George Burnside was, Mr Freeman. I hope you believe me. Kerry told me on Thursday evening about the way he treated Gina. Until then, I thought that all he was guilty of was hurting Nessie whenever he got drunk. Then, I realised that Grant treated Maggie in the same manner. I've seen the evidence with my eyes, and I'm ashamed to admit I ignored it. Gary's temper caused a different outcome. The children and Kirstin never suffered, thank goodness. He took his frustration and anger out on defenceless teenage boys."

"While you're in the mood to spill the beans, Iverson," said Gus, "do you have any information on who killed Grant?"

"You know the answer to that. I would have passed that knowledge on to Gary if I had discovered anything. But, no, neither of us found Grant's killer. They would have died by now if Gary learned who shot his father."

"What about Gary? Who was responsible for that?"

"Well, that might take you a while, Mr Freeman, because even with Gary dead, the Burnside reputation will make victims very wary of coming forward."

"I'm not investigating his murder," said Gus, "my consultancy role is purely for cold cases. Despite the lack of progress, I'm still hopeful we can find Grant's killer. We're not giving up yet."

"I wish you luck."

Gus thought Iverson had gone, but after a long pause, he was back.

"Do you have an address for Gina Burnside that I can pass to Kerry, Mr Freeman? Kerry thinks it's time to offer a helping hand."

"It might not be too late," said Gus, "and with the three

main tormentors now out of the picture, she might just stand a chance of life."

Gus told Patrick Iverson the street name and what he could remember of the boarded-up building.

Iverson ended the call.

"Are you ready for your lunch now," asked Suzie.

"I'd like to shower first, if I may. I want to wash the Burnside family out of my system."

Gus and Suzie travelled to the Waggon & Horses that evening for a meal. There was a band in the Stable Bar, and Suzie dragged Gus onto the small dance floor. It was fun for a while, but the gardening had tired him more than he cared to admit.

"You'll sleep well tonight," said Suzie as she drove them home.

"There's more work to do tomorrow," he replied.

Sunday proved to be a washout. Heavy showers prevented Gus from gardening, and Suzie persuaded him that an afternoon in bed was preferable to wandering in the rain just for exercise.

"I'm hungry," said Gus at seven in the evening.

"Well, you worked up an appetite," said Suzie, "I was most impressed."

"I know. I heard you. Shall I cook, or do you want to go out again?"

"I'll have a shower and consider," said Suzie, "back in five minutes."

Gus wandered into the lounge and waited. The phone rang. Typical. Gus wondered if it was Dorothy's friend. It worried him that she hadn't been in touch for ages.

"The Freeman household. How may I help?"

"Freeman, will you never grow up? It's Truelove here. Can I speak freely?"

"Was that a sneaky way of discovering whether I had company?" asked Gus. "Of course, you can. So what news do you have for me?"

"Gareth Francis called me from Gablecross."

"You're a sly one. I hadn't heard Gareth had unceremoniously transferred to one of your remote outposts."

"Nothing unceremonious about it. I thought it was the right move for DI Francis's career development. Look, I will not debate my decisions with you. He wants your help on this murder case you have embroiled yourself in. I told him I could spare you for forty-eight hours. Are you happy to work with him?"

"I'd be happier if I could wrap it up sooner," said Gus, giving Suzie a thumbs-up as she strolled into the lounge wrapped in a large bath towel. "I shall travel to Swindon in the morning. Please apologise to DS Mercer and the admin staff for not being at your ten o'clock meeting."

"There's nothing to report on the Grant Burnside murder yet anyway, I take it?" asked the ACC.

"We're chasing a rugged-looking, red-haired man in his thirties who enjoys climbing and outdoor pursuits–like hunting and shooting. Other than that, we've got nowhere."

"Goodnight, Freeman. Oh, and tell DI Ferris not to be late in the morning."

"Nice try, Sir," said Gus, "goodnight."

"You got your way, I assume?" asked Suzie.

"You know me. I keep nudging people until they take the sensible option."

"Don't I know it. Where shall we go to eat?" asked Suzie.

Gus wrapped his arms around her and removed the towel.

"I'll rustle us up a snack later," he said. "Sunday

evenings are always a reminder that you'll leave here in the morning, and I won't know when I'll see you again for days. It's painful."

Monday, 25 June 2018

"DO you have anything planned for this week?" asked Suzie.

"Are we talking social plans or work plans?" asked Gus, opening one eye.

Suzie was ready to leave for home. Another weekend was at an end.

"Bert's daughter, Margaret, will descend on the village with her nephew, Brett. I imagine we'll get an invitation to meet them during their visit. Once I hear specific dates and times, I'll call you."

"I look forward to it," said Suzie, "ring me tonight anyway. Bye."

With that, she disappeared. Gus rolled over to glance at the clock.

Yes, it was time to get up, shower and get dressed. Gus needed to get his brain into gear.

The past two days had been great, but all good things came to an end.

He had to drive to Gablecross Police Station to explain matters to DI Gareth Francis in an hour. Gus hoped that Jake Latimer was on hand to assist.

Before he left the bungalow, Gus called Neil Davis.

"Neil, I'm off to Swindon for a few hours. The ACC gave me the green light to hold Gareth's hand. I'll drive to Blunsdon at three o'clock if I cannot wrap things up this morning. I'll meet you and Luke there. He was getting the natty blue suits for the three of us. Double-check before you leave that they're in the car. I used mine on Friday."

"Leave it with me, guv," said Neil, "will you let us in on the secret?"

"Not yet, Neil. I might have screwed up. It wouldn't be the first time on this case. I thought Gina Burnside wasn't worth an interview, yet she held the key to everything. Everything except who killed her brother, of course."

"We'll see you at the pig farm then," said Neil.

Gus drove to Gablecross and found a spot in the visitor's car park. Unfortunately, nobody in Reception knew he was coming this morning, so he stood there like a lemon while the officer verified a DI Francis was on site.

"Sorry, Mr Freeman, he must be new. I guess you've been here before, so you know where the detective squad hangs out?"

Gus nodded and set off through the rabbit warren. He spotted Jake Latimer on the far side of the room. He had a desk near the window. Perhaps Jake was training for the ACC's job in a few years.

"Are you looking for Gareth?" asked Jake.

"The Acting Chief Constable called me yesterday evening to say DI Francis needed rescuing. So I'm on the clock. I need to nurse him through his first murder case before tomorrow's close of play."

"DI Francis is chasing forensics and any scraps of information that the Police Surgeon will feed him from the autopsy. Don't ask. I haven't heard a thing yet."

"What did Gareth ask you to do?" asked Gus.

"Come and have a look," said Jake. "The snooker club manager showed me the members' register from January 2017 to date. I've got eleven names to check. It won't take long. I've got mobile phone numbers for all, bar two of them and addresses for the others. So a landline could be available to simplify matters."

"There's always a chance that the eleven lads will claim they weren't involved, Jake," said Gus, "even though Gary's dead. As Patrick Iverson pointed out on Saturday afternoon, victims get frightened at the mention of the name Burnside."

"Do you think it will be too easy for them to bluff it out on the phone then, guv? Perhaps I should see them face-to-face. I might catch a telltale twitch."

"As long as it doesn't take too long," said Gus, "I've only got forty-eight hours. You haven't yet asked for the register of members for when Asif's uncle ran the place."

"Oh, I asked, guv," grinned Jake, "I'm collecting them at noon. Asif was picking them up from his uncle last night. So we'll have the period between January 2012 and December 2016 later."

"Good. I'll let you get stuck in to those addresses. At least they're local. Get on the phone and fix up a meeting. Some will be at work. Is there nobody to do the leg work for you?"

"I could grab PCSO Travers for two hours," said Jake, "nobody knows what to do with him. He's green as grass."

"Travers was certainly green on Friday afternoon," said Gus. "Oh, there was something I thought of at the weekend. Neil and Luke spoke with Simeon Young on Friday. Does his name appear in that register?"

"He's one of my eleven names, guv," said Jake, checking the list.

"You need to chase over to Malmesbury to catch Simeon between inventions," said Gus, "he's one of the Burnside dropouts that's turned over a new leaf."

"I'll start making these calls and then see whether I can

use Travers to pick up the register of members for those missing years from Asif. Travers has been to the club, so he shouldn't get lost."

"I'll get back to see you this afternoon before I leave, Jake. We're visiting Farmer McHugh out at Blunsdon."

"I don't envy you that job, guv," said Jake, "I get the shivers just thinking about it."

"This won't help then," said Gus. "Iverson confessed that Grant and Gary killed at least twelve people in the past eight years."

"That's a lot of caustic soda," said Jake. "I looked it up one night when I was at a loose end. Dissolving bodies in lye is a tried and trusted method used by the Mexican Sinaloa drug cartel to eliminate corpses. Fergus McHugh needed around a hundred pounds of powdered lye to dissolve a body."

"I'll remember to ask him where he bought his supplies, Jake," said Gus, heading for the door.

Gus thought it might be quicker to find his way back to Reception than wander around the many corridors in this building. He spotted the same officer on the desk and called him over.

"DI Francis is with the Police Surgeon discussing a recent autopsy. Can you point me in the right direction?"

"You won't believe me, but it's Room 101," said the officer.

"Which direction?"

"Head along the main corridor and look for the numbers by the stairwells. You can't miss them."

He was right. Gus was outside the door in two minutes. He could see Gareth Francis, head bowed. Was he praying or napping?

Gus knocked and entered. As soon as he set foot inside

the room, he heard a female voice. Was that the Police Surgeon? If so, where was she?

Gareth raised his finger to his lips, showing that Gus should button it.

Gus thought this was different. It appeared this station was one of those the ACC referred to that used a GP part-time. Everyone who lived in Swindon knew how difficult it was to get to see a Doctor. Even Gareth couldn't get to see her face-to-face.

Dr Northwood did her bit and recorded it for posterity. Gareth was listening to her report.

Gareth handed Gus the first two sheets of notes he'd summarised.

Dr Eve Northwood had attended the scene at one o'clock.

The estimated time of death was between ten to twelve hours earlier.

The disposition of the body and its surroundings matched what Gus witnessed.

The body had been identified one hour earlier by Augustus John Freeman.

Eve Northwood had made a preliminary examination of the body in situ.

At four o'clock, Gary Burnside's body was moved to the mortuary.

At the post-mortem, which Dr Northwood carried out before her morning surgery, she determined the cause of death.

The deceased received twelve stab wounds from four different bladed weapons. There were seven wounds to the rear of the torso and five to the front. Additionally, all major organs suffered at least one puncturing wound.

Gus turned over the first sheet to see Gareth's sketched

body plan, showing where each entry occurred. When Dr Northwood referred to the sequence of the attacks, she stressed it was difficult to determine the order in which they occurred.

Her professional opinion was that four assailants had struck Burnside simultaneously in a brief but bloody attack.

When she removed the broken snooker cue butt from the victim's rectum, it appeared that its role was to force a round object further into Gary Burnside's back passage.

Dr Northwood had ordered further tests to confirm at what point death occurred during the assault. It was unclear whether the insertion of the round object (which measured fifty-two-point-five millimetres in diameter) occurred pre or post-mortem. She believed the cue butt entered the victim's body post-mortem.

After its removal, Dr Northwood identified the round object as a snooker ball. Behind the black ball was a slip of paper, which she removed with tweezers.

The slip of paper contained a list of names.

Gareth Francis was still holding his last sheet of notes. Gus was eager to see the contents of that list.

Gus listened to Eve Northwood as she stated that police did not recover any sharp-bladed weapons matching the wounds at the scene. Her summation didn't vary much from Gus's assessment. Finally, the room fell silent, and Gareth walked to a nearby desk and switched off the machine.

"Can I see that list of names, Gareth?" asked Gus.

"It's still getting analysed," said Gareth, "I suppose we must be thankful that they can read it at all."

"Statistically, only ten per cent of bodies suffer from the scenario you're painting. You stood beside me and viewed Gary Burnside's body. The massive blood loss left us coping with that coppery, pungent odour that catches inexperienced officers such as that young PCSO. But whoever murdered Gary Burnside, and rammed those additional items into his body, unintentionally spared us the worst outcome."

"I remember our chat at London Road," said Gareth, "after the autopsy I attended with Peter Morgan. Peter gave me far more information than I wanted to know on the subject. I was so keen to learn and couldn't contain my excitement. Until he went into great detail about what happened to the body after death."

"Yes, Gary Burnside's muscles relaxed, and no doubt something escaped into the air in that Matchroom, but the overriding smell ten hours after death was from his blood. Your Police Surgeon appears to have recovered a vital piece of evidence. Did you transcribe the names from the recording? You did a good job on the rest of it. The killing went pretty much as I thought, but I couldn't see the entry wounds on his back. The four attackers surrounded him, and he didn't stand a chance."

"That slip of paper suffered discolouration and tearing. We must wait until it's processed. There may have been one other person in the room that we have yet to identify."

"Well done, Gareth," said Gus. "Gary's final victim. Perhaps Asif can help with that, as he was there until midnight. Also, Asif should know which junior members were present that night. If Gary booked the Matchroom and sent Asif home, then it's odds on he had company."

"I wonder why the lad hasn't come forward?" asked Gareth.

"Why didn't any of Gary's victims come forward?" said Gus. "Shame and fear of reprisals from the Burnside gang would explain the silence of his past victims. But the young lad who was face down on the snooker table Thursday night when the attackers broke in witnessed at least the first stabbings. Did he stay and watch, or did they tell him to get out and tell no one what he'd seen?"

"It might be difficult to persuade anyone to speak about such an ordeal. Especially when a group of vigilantes burst in and do what the victim wanted to do himself."

"Let's not get ahead of ourselves," said Gus. "DS Latimer is chasing potential victims from the latest register of members and was hoping to get PCSO Travers to assist with identifying youngsters using the club three or four years ago."

"Should I ring him and stop what he's doing?" asked Gareth.

"If that list Dr Northwood recovered is accurate, then Jake's task isn't urgent. It still needs doing, but only a proportion of the eleven names from the past eighteen months will appear on the list. So we must regroup and devise a revised plan of action."

Gareth nodded. They returned to the detective squad room to look for Jake Latimer.

"He's visiting addresses in Blunsdon, Gorse Hill, Pinehurst, and Highworth," said a colleague.

"Where would we find PCSO Travers?" asked Gareth.

"Not a clue, Gareth. He's doing something for Jake. He left here about ten minutes ago and said he'd be back around half-past twelve."

"Jake's sent him to the closest addresses on the first list, and then he's collecting the lists of members when Asif's uncle was in charge. So we should call them both back."

"Not to worry, Gareth," said Gus, "leave them for now. Get hold of Asif's number and tell him to meet us at the club in the next ten minutes. Then, we'll collect the register and get a head start finding our killers."

"I don't follow," said Gareth.

"Come on, Gareth, you've been doing so well," sighed Gus. "Who would know the victims' names and want to kill their attacker?"

"They could be fathers of boys he attacked," suggested Gareth.

"True, but they could also be club members who used the place regularly and saw what was going on."

"And they must have been members for several years if the names of *all* the victims are on the list they left inside Burnside."

"Exactly," said Gus.

Gareth called Asif, and he met them outside the snooker club. He had his uncle's books with him.

"Many thanks, Asif," said Gus, "sorry to get you here earlier, but these records could hold vital information."

"No problem, Mr Freeman. I can always use the extra time clearing the Matchroom now your forensic people have done with it. My two new pool tables will be here next week."

"I like a man who doesn't let the grass grow under his feet," said Gus, "you'll turn this place around, Asif. I'd put money on it."

"It won't be for lack of trying, Mr Freeman."

"Can you remember the names of any youngsters here last Thursday, Asif? Do you know who was receiving one-to-one coaching from Gary Burnside?"

"There weren't many in on Thursday. Emilio Melillo and Kendal Andrews were playing on Table 3. I didn't see Emilio leave."

"Was he the better player of the two?" asked Gus.

"Oh yes, he's good at most sports," said Asif.

"We'll find him," said Gareth, "thanks for your help."

As he turned to leave, Gus remembered the young PCSO.

"That young lad, Travers, was here on Friday, Asif. He'll be here at noon looking for these books. Send him back to the police station, will you? Apologise for getting here before him."

"Will do, Mr Freeman," said Asif, moving towards the club door to open up.

Gareth and Gus returned to Gablecross. Unfortunately, there was still no sign of Jake Latimer.

"What period do these books cover?" asked Gareth.

"The five years between January 2012 and December 2016," said Gus.

"I see they still use the same type of register," said Gareth, pointing to the two books on Jake Latimer's desk.

"How are the names listed?" asked Gus.

"For each day the club was open, there's a record of who joined, with their address, contact number, and annual fee payable. It's a different amount for under-18s, adults, and senior citizens. There are dozens of names recorded in January. So, they include people who were members the previous year. Ah, I see what they do now. In February, the annual fee rises. That encourages existing members to pay their fees in the New Year to save themselves twenty per cent."

"Good, that makes our job easier. I'll take the first book," said Gus. "You grab the 2018 book from Jake's desk. Make a list of names of adults who joined in January this year. Then go back to 2017 and check the names that re-occur. We'll put our lists together and see how many long-term members use the snooker club. Our killers will be among those names."

Gus and Gareth worked their way through the seven registers for the next hour.

The door of the detective squad room opened at around twelve-fifteen, and in strode Jake Latimer.

"Just in time, Jake," said Gareth, "we're almost ready for you."

"What's going on?" asked Jake, "when did those extra books appear? I didn't think Travers would be back yet. He had several addresses to visit in Broadgreen first."

Gus explained what they had done and why.

"I could have saved myself that legwork if I'd waited to hear the autopsy findings. Sorry, boss."

"That's life, Jake," said Gareth, "it's good experience. Travers will learn something from this, too. He should walk through that door in a minute. We've still got one year to check, and then we can compare results."

"What can I do to help?" asked Jake.

"The most important piece of the jigsaw," said Gus, "dig out the murder file for Blake Dixon. Give me the names of the four lads playing on Table 7 that night."

"What, the ones who got struck dumb when questioned about what happened?"

"The very same. I want to see whether those four continued to play at the club after 2013, despite the hassle."

PCSO Travers returned at half-past twelve and handed Jake the information he had gathered on his Broadgreen walkabout.

"Do you need me for anything else, Sir?" he asked Jake.

"I don't know. Do I?" Jake asked, looking at Gus and Gareth.

"Travers can collate the information you both gathered on your travels. Then, this afternoon, he can drill through these earlier books to uncover the other potential victims.

It's a chore, but it will help once you've isolated a series of names that we can compare with the slip of paper Dr Northwood's keeping safe."

"What time are you leaving?" asked Jake.

"How long will it take me to get to Blunsdon?"

"It's a ten-minute drive to McHugh's farm if you're lucky."

"I'll stay here for another ninety minutes. But, first, let's get these annual registers finalised."

The three detectives sat around Jake's desk and compared their results.

"Does this remind you of Happy Families?" asked Jake.

"Not really," said Gareth.

"I'll start," said Gus, "Wayne Stuart joined on January the eleventh, 2012.

"I got him in 2015," said Jake.

"He rejoined this year," said Gareth.

"Wayne was twenty in 2012. Right, Jake, where's that Blake Dixon murder file?"

"I sent Travers to collect it. He won't be long. Let's hope it didn't get lost."

Gareth and Gus shared a glance. Fingers crossed.

PCSO Travers returned with the 2013 murder file. They could breathe again.

"Travers, make yourself useful," said Gus. "Dig through the sheets in that file. Find the details of the four lads in the snooker club late that night. Their interviews were brief, but I hope someone remembered to record their names."

"Shall I give you another name from my 2012 register?" Gus asked Gareth and Jake.

"Found it," cried young Travers. "Jason Dean, 22; Liam Winter, 23; Rob Coleman, 23; and Wayne Stuart, 21."

"Bingo!" cried Gus. "Do we have a match every year since?"

"We do," echoed Gareth and Jake.

"Why do you think they're the killers, guv?" said Jake, turning to Gus.

"Gareth?" asked Gus.

"Don't look at me. I'm still catching up."

PCSO Travers spoke next.

"If they were in the club playing snooker from the same age as the young lads I talked to this morning, they knew what was going on. When Dixon got murdered in the Matchroom, these four were outside in the games room. They must have been scared that the gang would punish them, but all they got was waived table fees, a free bottle of Bud, and a verbal warning. They've held onto the thought they should have spoken out for five years. Think of the number of youngsters Gary Burnside could have raped in that time. Last Thursday night was the last straw."

"Neither of those four was in the club on Thursday," said Jake, checking the register.

"Then it was personal," said PCSO Travers,

"Go on, Travers, you've got it worked out this far. Tie it up in a neat bow," said Gus.

"You had already worked it out, hadn't you?" said Gareth.

"I still want to see the names on that list that they inserted into Gary Burnside," said Gus.

"Was it Emilio that proved to be the final straw?" asked Travers.

"If there's a link between one of our four suspects and Emilio Melillo," said Gareth Francis. "we'd better find it, and we'll be ready to bring them in."

Travers was flicking through his mobile phone.

"It's Wayne Stuart, Sir. He's engaged to Maria Melillo. Emilio is her younger brother."

"Facebook?" asked Gus.

"Instagram," said Travers.

"Where would we be without social media," said Gus getting out of his chair and preparing to leave,

"Where are you off to?" asked Gareth.

"I'm off to search for a decent place for a lunchtime snack before I drive out to Blunsdon. The three of you have got most of what you need to prepare a case against your four suspects. Those further tests that Dr Northwood ordered will give you more answers that might lessen the hurt for the Burnside family. That soiled paper will reveal the exact number of Gary Burnside's victims. I wish you luck getting those victims to open up and tell you details of their ordeal. Get them any counselling they require. I hadn't connected the last victim and the group of four, but it explains why Emilio didn't come forward. They didn't need to warn him not to say anything. Why would he drop his future brother-in-law in it?"

"The Burnside legacy lives on," said Jake. "For decades, they've ruled the roost in town and ruined the lives of dozens of people. Even with Grant and Gary dead, it still goes on. Now we've got to arrest four young men in their mid-twenties for murder. That's something their families will carry with them for decades."

"I can't have too much sympathy for them, Jake," said Gus. "They didn't speak out when they could have, and frustration and anger at their weakness festered until someone close to them got threatened. Imagine if Kendal Andrews was the better player of the two lads in that club last Thursday."

Gus Freeman left the detective squad room and headed

for the front door. Where was that place he'd bought a snack when he was up here last?

Chapter Twelve

AFTER A HEARTY LUNCH, Gus Freeman made his way towards Blunsdon on the A419.

He pondered the wisdom of visiting Fergus McHugh's farm on a full stomach.

Gus turned off the main road onto the track that led to the farm and spotted Luke's car ahead. The lads were here; they didn't have to hang around too long.

"How did it go this morning, guv?" asked Neil.

"As expected, Neil," Gus replied.

"The boss won't tell you yet, Neil," said Luke, "he'll give you a few scraps of information and hope you piece it together yourself."

"Let's get changed into these natty blue suits, gentlemen," said Gus, "as for the Gary Burnside case, you had better pull your socks up. A wet-behind-the-ears PCSO worked it out before Jake Latimer and Gareth Francis."

"I can understand Gareth not getting it, guv," said Neil, slipping on his knee-high wellington boots. "I expected better from Jake Latimer."

"Where's Fergus McHugh?" asked Gus, "I thought he'd be at the farmhouse door awaiting your arrival."

"McHugh's in the barn already, guv," said Luke. "we're to join him inside when we're ready."

The elderly farmer looked up at the three blue figures in the doorway.

"They're both dead now," he said.

Gus looked at the steel contraption in front of him.

"Has he just completed another disposal job?"

"No, guv," said Neil, "I think he wants to come clean."

"Grant and Gary," said Fergus, "they're both dead now. I met Grant in a pub, agreed to work for him, and purchased caustic soda from hardware shops. A curious shop owner once asked me why I needed so much. I told the woman that I used it to clean my farmhouse. I didn't enjoy working for Gary these past four years. He was an objectionable swine. I'd had enough of it."

"It must have been a disgusting task, Mr McHugh," said Luke.

"It was routine to me," said McHugh. "They brought me the packages, and I just got rid of them. I didn't ask what was inside. I don't feel I did anything wrong. It was just a service I provided."

Neil inspected the equipment and the surrounding area. Then, finally, McHugh pointed to the rank of trees on the hillside. "That's where I lit the fires," he said. "There's nothing left now."

Neil and Luke drove up to look.

Gus stood and watched with Fergus McHugh.

"What will happen to me now?" asked McHugh.

"This has to be the strangest case I've ever investigated," said Gus. "I got tasked with finding out who killed Grant Burnside. I've helped solve several crimes but have not found a clue that's yet gotten me closer to success in that task. As for you and this barn behind me, it was used to dispose of at least a dozen dead bodies. You've done your work so well that there's no evidence left against you. If I was interested in punishing you for your role in that business, Sylvia Kerr's complaint about the frequent bonfires is the only thing left. I might charge you with creating a public nuisance. That's not why I came out of retirement. I want to solve cold cases. I wish you luck selling this place, Mr McHugh. We'll get off your land when my lads have finished up there on the hillside."

Tuesday, 26 June 2018

GUS LEFT the bungalow and drove towards Devizes. There was no need to bother Gablecross today. DI Francis and DS Latimer had their hands full, but Gus thought they would cope. In two years, they might look over their shoulder at young Travers snapping at their coattails.

Who would have thought he'd get a grip of the essentials so quickly? It's the modern way to use social media to make connections. That was what Geoff Mercer reckoned the much-vaunted Hub was supposed to provide.

They offered nothing helpful in this case. In fairness, the team didn't ask the Hub's whiz kids a single question. Could the Hub throw up a name for Grant Burnside's killer? Gus toyed with the idea of popping into London Road but opted instead to drive straight to the Old Police Station office. There were loose ends to tie up there first.

When he exited the lift, the transformed layout surprised him. After they drove back from Blunsdon yesterday afternoon, he'd gone straight home. But instead, Luke and Neil had come here to see what Lydia had coaxed the furniture guys to achieve.

Gus had to admit she'd done an excellent job.

Alex's desk was unmoved, and Lydia now sat behind him. That seemed fair enough.

Luke's desk was now where Neil used to be. Neil was behind him next to the restroom door. Blessing Umeh was to sit in the middle of the room where Lydia used to be. It might help her feel welcome and surrounded by the team instead of getting stuck on a limb.

Next week would be another new beginning. Gus had never managed a team this big when he worked full time, certainly not for day-to-day matters. Unless they were on a murder case, he was lucky to have two Sergeants reporting to him. Now, he had three, plus a Detective Constable and a university graduate.

It was heady stuff. Gus hadn't imagined his retirement this way.

Gus heard the lift descend to the ground floor. The others were on their way.

Wrong again. It was Geoff Mercer.

"I thought I should drop by to see where my money went," said Geoff.

"We're still waiting on the delivery for the super-fast thingy and the new-fangled doofer," said Gus.

"Dream on," said Geoff. "Mine has been on order for months. But, unfortunately, the factory can't keep pace with demand."

"Joking apart, we're grateful," said Gus. "This setup will work for the time being. Luke added two pieces of hardware to the list we could use if our workload remains high."

"Gablecross would have first dibs on that kit, I imagine,"

said Geoff. "The work you've done off-task in the past week has given them more than enough to handle. I don't know how you do it, Gus."

"Good, old-fashioned police work," said Gus. "Keep asking questions and listen to the answers."

"We heard from Bridgend yesterday. Rhys Evans will reach us at the end of July."

"Did the ACC have any joy finding him a place to rest his weary Welsh head?"

"Kenneth did as you suggested," said Geoff, "he called Monty Jennings. Rhys Evans has a billet in Worton. One hundred yards up the road from Kassie Trotter."

"Everything comes to she who waits," said Gus. "I wonder if he likes cake?"

"And hearts and lovebirds," said Geoff.

The lift was in action once more. This time it was the Three Musketeers who arrived through the lift doors.

"I hope you don't want something back, Sir," said Lydia.

"Not likely, Lydia," grinned Geoff. "I just wanted a chat with your boss."

Luke, Neil, and Lydia set to work. They knew the score. Gus hadn't given the word yet, but everything they collected on the Burnside family last week should get collated and forwarded to detectives at Gablecross.

They started work on that on Friday afternoon, despite the mess the furniture crew was clearing up around them. Soon, that element of the case would leave them, and the Freeman Files needed updating. Sadly, little of what they had entered related to Grant Burnside's murder.

Perhaps, once DS Mercer left for London Road, Gus could give them a new direction.

"You wanted to chat and check that we hadn't pinched an extra chair?"

"I was thinking of Grant Burnside," said Geoff. "The ACC mentioned that you reckoned a red-haired man in his thirties might have been the sniper. He doesn't ring any bells with me. Do you remember that chat in the Bear before you started working here? I mentioned the inter-gang slaughter that took place in this town. What, seventeen years ago now? There were similarities with the Burnside affair."

"In what way?" asked Gus.

"The leaders and senior figures of both gangs died that night. We believed that with the head of the snake gone, we would make significant progress in mopping up the low-level criminals floundering without leadership."

"I remember you saying that they soon lost the initiative because of the weak direction from our masters."

"There was always a suspicion that it wasn't the two gangs striking out at one another. The ACC wondered whether Burnside was another example. Why did we find no clues? If one of the other known gangs involved in drugs in Swindon did it, why didn't we find the connection?"

"I had an interesting conversation with Jack Sanders the other morning," said Gus. "He came at it a different way. Jack's niggle was a case in 2012 where four leaders of a grooming gang vanished. Was it another example of someone removing the head of the snake? The whole sordid business collapsed within days of those fours' disappearance."

"What's your take on it?" asked Geoff.

"Luke had the right question to answer," said Gus. "Who could know where Grant would be that morning? Of course, I'd be a fool to say that phones didn't get tapped and listening devices installed in cars, homes, and offices, but who would be responsible?"

"It sounds far-fetched to me," said Geoff, "I'd better get back to London Road. Vera Butler is back at work, by the way. She's feeling better."

"Glad to hear it," said Gus, "before you go, can I ask a favour?"

"Sure," said Geoff.

"Can I let the team have time off this week? There might be fewer opportunities after our newbies join us. We'll wrap up the last bits of the different Burnside matters today. Then, I'll drop in to see you and the ACC with my recommendations regarding Grant's murder. It might warrant another look at a later date unless we can work out how our mystery man learned so much about Grant Burnside's itinerary."

"There's no shortage of cases for you to handle, Gus. Perhaps the Hub can start search routines for you. Give them a few weeks to identify possible names for your sniper, and then pick the case up again. You'll have several pairs of hands to keep occupied from next week. You know how to juggle, don't you?"

"You're all heart, Geoff," said Gus, "but it makes sense. I don't like quitting on a case."

"Don't worry about the ACC," said Geoff, "you got enough unexpected results from this cold case review for Gablecross to be eternally grateful. There are still plenty of green ticks against the CRT's name. I'll see you in the morning. Goodbye, all."

With that, Geoff Mercer left the building.

"Do we have any more loose ends to tidy up, guv?" asked Luke.

"I'll run through the Freeman Files and see what you

three have added since Friday," said Gus. "I haven't caught up with everything yet. Then, I'll add my reports and pass the relevant bits onto Gablecross. The ball is in their court now."

Gus stepped through the digital record of what happened since the ACC handed him the Grant Burnside murder file.

His first interview had been with Maggie, Grant's widow. What a sorry state she would be in now.

Her father-in-law, George, wanted his legacy to be a Burnside dynasty based on a solid family base, where everyone stuck together, no matter what.

Did George's wife, Nessie, know what happened between George and Gina? Maybe not, but Maggie knew because Grant expressed relief when George died. Grant feared for the safety of Kerry, his only daughter.

Maggie also knew her eldest son, Gary, had a violent temper. Her sister-in-law, Gina, told her on more than one occasion. Gus had learned what happened to Gary in prison and how Maggie's troubled son killed a dozen men when his violent temper surfaced. So she had that to contend with, plus Gary was savagely attacking several young men in the snooker club. But, of course, he didn't believe she knew anything about that.

If Kerry's analysis of Kirstin were correct, Maggie would soon lose her companion. Then, Kirstin and the only grandchildren Maggie had would be off to pastures new.

Henry and Joseph faced arrest and incarceration. Patrick Iverson might shield them from the murders carried out by Grant and Gary, but drug trafficking and dealing carry a high tariff. They were both going away for a long time.

Gus wondered what would happen to Vic Hodge and Kerry Burnside.

The telephone rang.

"Mr Freeman, it's Gareth Francis here,"

"Good morning, Gareth. I thought I'd done enough for you yesterday. What's up?"

"Nothing," said Gareth, "I wanted to thank you and tell you I received a phone call yesterday afternoon after you left. DS Latimer is at HMP Bristol as we speak. Vic Hodge is singing like a bird. I'm driving to see Ms Burnside after this call. She's eager to talk with us too."

"It couldn't be better news, Gareth. Go easy on her, won't you? Her heart's in the right place."

"Will do," said Gareth, "I look forward to working with you again."

Gus hung up before he said something he regretted.

Gus thought that maybe he needn't worry too much about Vic and Kerry. They might escape from this mess without too much damage. According to Patrick Iverson, Kerry made the first approach to Gina yesterday, so that was one lost sheep that could return to the fold.

Gus looked up to see what Lydia was doing.

She sensed someone watching her and glanced over the top of her computer screen.

"Are you okay, guv?" she asked.

"Do you remember our visit to Maggie's house?"

"How could I forget? She looked like death behind that haze of smoke, but she didn't want a single material thing. So instead, she surrounded herself with those items most dear to her."

"What did you call them? Her creature comforts, wasn't it?" said Gus.

"Yes," said Lydia, "but things have changed beyond recognition since then, haven't they?

"What Maggie learns in the coming weeks concerning those family members whose photos surround her, she might consider them creature discomforts, not comforts."

Gus completed his recommendations for the ACC and looked up to see Lydia bringing him a coffee.

"Just what I needed," he said.

When Lydia returned to her desk, he suddenly remembered something.

Gus opened his desk drawer and found the Bourbon biscuit he'd kept back for a special occasion. Of course, there was nothing to celebrate, but so what.

Next in The Freeman Files series

vinci-books.com/silentterror

Silent terror, haunting secrets.

In the heart of Wiltshire, a chilling mystery resurfaces as Gus Freeman and his newly expanded Crime Review Team delve into the haunting murder of Ursula Wakeley, a spinster librarian.

Turn the page for a free preview…

Silent Terror: Prologue

Growing up in Dundee, Lydia Logan's childhood was a happy one. She always knew she was adopted but didn't give it much thought. Her mother, Eleanor Scott, was eighteen when she gave birth to a seven pounds eleven-ounce daughter. The record for her father showed him merely as a Nigerian sailor from Lagos.

Lydia's parents agreed to a closed adoption, which meant few details were made available. Her parents hadn't even known her birth mother's name. When Lydia left school at eighteen, she wanted to be an actress and worked several jobs to fund her classes at Drama school in Glasgow.

Lydia spent years badgering the adoption agency and adoption support groups. While she studied, she spent countless hours in libraries searching the internet. Alex Hardy knew it must have been a tough time for both Lydia and her parents. Despite the loving childhood the Logan's

215

provided, he appreciated Lydia's desire to meet the man and woman who brought her into the world.

Lydia had stayed in digs in term time in Glasgow while she studied, returning home during the holidays. When she reached twenty-one, she moved out for good. The only way Lydia could continue to finance her studies was to work year-round, even if it was part-time. There was no animosity with her parents. Lydia knew she could give them a ring, and her bed would be ready before she'd made the ninety-minute trip back to Dundee.

While she sat in the Mitchell Library searching for a way to find her father, she wondered which occupation might offer the most access to information impossible to unlock online. Lydia hunted for books on forensic psychology and read them to fill in time between internet searches for her father without raising red flags.

Lydia switched her focus to an MSc in Forensic Psychology at Glasgow Caledonian University once she decided this leg of the hunt for her father required a more structured approach.

There were bound to have been pressures on both sides. At the outset, Lydia did not understand why the young Eleanor Scott gave her daughter up for adoption. Was it just the economic impact of caring for a baby alone? The father had disappeared within days of that first meeting, and she'd never heard from again. Inevitably, he never learned he'd fathered a child. Would Eleanor welcome her daughter getting in touch? How would that impact the Logan family if the pair formed a relationship?

Lydia's persistence got its reward in time. The adoption agency wrote to tell her she was now entitled to learn her birth name. Eleanor Scott had named her Lisa Marie.

Armed with this extra knowledge, Lydia then questioned her motives for wanting to continue the hunt.

What if she contacted Eleanor and her mother didn't want to meet her? When Lydia finally plucked up the courage to make that call to Eleanor, it was through a mediator. Lydia stressed that she wasn't asking for anything from Eleanor but was curious to learn more about her. They talked from time to time on the phone for several months before either was ready to meet in person. When they did meet face-to-face, they found it easier to behave as friends rather than attempt to force an instant bond.

When Alex and Lydia got together, she told him what had happened at that first meeting and the information she had gained.

The eighteen-year-old Eleanor Scott worked in a gift shop on George Street, Edinburgh. She started there straight from school. Lydia learned that her father was Chidozie Barre, aged twenty-one, from Yaba, near Lagos.

Chidozie had arrived in the port of Leith two days before he met Eleanor. He was on shore leave for five days and entered the gift shop searching for a memory of Scotland to take home to his mother. The young sailor asked Eleanor to meet him later that evening.

"Chi-Chi, his friends called him," Eleanor had told Lydia. "He was tall and handsome. His smile lit up the shop. I wasn't seeing anyone else, so I thought, why not? When I left work, he waited for me outside. His friends had returned to the ship. We walked to the George IV pub, Chi-Chi bought us a drink, and then we went to the cinema. Please don't ask me what was showing. I can't remember. I told him I needed to get home because my parents didn't know I was staying in the city after work. He was a gentleman. Chi-Chi walked me to the bus stop, and we met the next evening. At half-past five, I came outside the shop, and there he was with a single red rose. We revisited the pub and stayed longer this time. I wasn't a big drinker, so my head was spinning when we came outside. We went to Princes Street Gardens. That was when it happened. I knew he was leaving the next day, and we wouldn't have another night together. It was the first time for both of us. I caught the last bus home and cried myself to sleep. Not because of what we did or because we didn't use protection. It was because I realised that I'd never see him again. My heart sank when I missed that first period. What could I do? I knew his name, but where did he go after he left Leith? What was the name of the ship? It never seemed important to ask. My family didn't want to know. It would have been bad enough if it had been Geordie McEwan from next door. He'd always kept asking for a date, but I was not too fond of the sight of him. But when my Dad heard it was a black man, that was it. I was out the door with my belongings and looking for digs."

Lydia had asked her mother how she'd coped and why she chose the name Lisa Marie.

"The gift shop manager was smashing. She had a cousin with a room for rent, and I worked behind the counter until I grew too big and had to stop. Giving you a name was the only thing I could do before you got taken away from me. Elvis's daughter was pregnant then, and I saw her name in the newspaper that day. I didn't think I would ever see you again, but how hard could it be if I looked for a Lisa Marie?"

Lydia explained to Eleanor how her adoptive parents came to name her Lydia. Not that they didn't approve of her given name of Lisa Marie, or they wanted to prevent

Eleanor from finding her if she came looking. Lydia was her adoptive father's mother's name. It was as simple as that.

So, Eleanor and Lydia kept in touch, primarily by phone. After she completed her MSc, Lydia travelled south for an interview at London Road. Then, she returned to Dundee to visit her parents while she awaited the verdict. They were over the moon when the ACC rang with the news that Wiltshire Police wanted Lydia to start work on April the ninth. Her parents stood on the doorstep with tears in their eyes when Lydia drove away in her red Mini. Lydia was tearful, too, because all three of them accepted that things would never be the same.

When she stepped from her Dundee home on Thursday, the fifth of April, Lydia had just informed her parents she was now Lydia Logan Barre. She drove south to collect the keys to her newly rented accommodation near Chippenham, eager to join the newly formed Crime Review Team on Monday. Little did she know that one of her teammates would become so important to her within a few weeks.

Lydia took the train to Edinburgh on Thursday, the tenth of May, and spent the weekend with Eleanor in Craigmillar. Eleanor had lived in that vibrant part of the city for ten years. They spent the time sightseeing and shopping and got on fine.

Lydia didn't want to spoil the mood. She told Eleanor of her new love, Alex, and how much she enjoyed working with Gus Freeman, even if he occasionally criticised her choice of clothing. As she travelled south on a gruelling train journey on Sunday, she thought about what she hadn't shared with her mother.

She didn't tell Eleanor of her attempts to trace her father. Eleanor hadn't forgotten her first love, but she'd moved on. Lydia planned to continue the search for

Chidozie Barre with Alex's help. Her father might not want to see her. But, if he did and asked after Eleanor, that was the right time to ask Elcanor if she wished Chidozie to get in touch. She would leave it to Eleanor to decide.

Lydia and Alex had discussed the next steps they needed to take. First, they had to find the ship he arrived on and where it went when it left the Port of Leith. It was something Lydia said she had to do. She couldn't rest until she found him. It was essential for Lydia to know the man who made her the person she was today.

Alex warned her she wouldn't find it easy to trace Chidozie through Police records unless he now lived in the UK and had committed an offence. Without a valid reason, Lydia couldn't just log on and start searching. Someone would notice.

Lydia knew Alex would do everything he could to help her in her quest. She was glad he was with her today to encourage her to keep going and make sure she did nothing illegal in her haste to find answers.

They had driven to London last night and stayed in a hotel near Greenwich. The Tube journey on the Jubilee Line to the National Maritime Museum took twenty minutes. The person she talked to was knowledgeable, but Lydia realised how challenging this task might be the more she listened.

"How do I trace a ship?" Lydia had asked the Maritime Museum assistant.

"Sometimes, the only way to trace a seaman's record is to trace the records of the ships on which he sailed. You can use the Crew List Index Project website to trace a ship by its name and port of registration. That can help locate merchant seamen in service up to the last decades of the twentieth century."

"Do the seamen have to be British to appear?" asked Lydia.

"Not necessarily, they recorded seamen serving on British registered vessels, but the men themselves need not have been British to appear in the records. Your father visited Leith in the early Nineties, you say?"

"In late ninety-two, that's right."

"It might be better to check the Maritime and Coast-guard Agency. That records seamen after 1972. If he was only employed temporarily or was an apprentice, he may not have had a British Seaman's Identity Card, in which case he's unlikely to appear in either register."

"I can still look, though. I want to find my Dad."

"Access to full details of seamen born less than one hundred years ago may be restricted."

"The CLIP catalogues are arranged alphabetically in ranges of surnames. The registers are in eight parts according to the nationality or origin of the seamen and other criteria. It allows for more targeted browsing. You can drill down to what's often referred to as the seaman's docket book. The docket book will show their date and place of birth, rank, or rating. A list of ships and their official numbers with date and place of engagement. It should highlight whether the engagement was for a Foreign or Home trade voyage. Finally, it will include the date and place of discharge from the ship."

Lydia left the Help desk and returned to find Alex.

"Any luck?" he asked.

"It's a shame Gus wants us back at work on Monday," she sighed. "It's a far bigger job than I hoped."

"I'm here to help," said Alex. "We can make a start between now and Friday. If we have to spend our weekends hunting your Dad, that's what we'll do. I know it's important to you."

"You're right," said Lydia, "I've waited twenty-five years to speak to him. Another few weeks won't make that much difference."

Armed with the information Lydia gleaned, the pair set to work on the National Archives. Hours passed, and when the Museum was closing, they realised they needed to return in the morning.

Despite too many drinks in the West End the previous night, Alex and Lydia returned to resume their search by ten the following day.

"It's like peeling away the layers of an onion one at a time, isn't it?" said Lydia.

"You're not kidding," said Alex. "What does your Dad's name mean, anyway? Do you know?"

"I looked it up like an obedient daughter," said Lydia. "May God fix it and make it good for you."

"Right," said Alex, "I might have found something. Perhaps he's fixed it for us. Did you know that refrigerated cargo made up twelve per cent of the goods carried on the seas back in 1992?"

"Before my time," said Lydia.

"Harsh," said Alex, "I was at school, but I wasn't studying economics. Seaborne trade continued to expand despite the downward path of the world economy at the start of the Nineties. One of the major shipping nations back then was Greece, and they remain in the Top Five today. I've found a ship they term a Reefer which transports perishable commodities which require temperature-controlled transportation, such as fruit, meat, fish, vegetables, and dairy products."

"Let me see," said Lydia.

"Don't get too excited," said Alex, "this only gets us part of the way to your father. A Greek ship, sailing under a foreign flag, docked in the Port of Leith between the days your mother mentioned. That reefer was six years old."

"What does sailing under a foreign flag mean?" asked Lydia.

"It's complicated, and it doesn't affect the aim of your search. In simple terms, most merchant ships flying a foreign flag belong to foreign owners who wish to avoid the stricter marine regulations imposed by their own countries. A foreign flag can offer easier registration and the ability to use cheaper foreign labour. Furthermore, foreign owners pay no income taxes."

"What was this ship called?" asked Lydia.

"It carried an Automatic Identification System named CB3 Reefer for location and identification. They built it in 1986, one hundred and thirty-four metres in length and twenty metres wide. Its call sign was 4FKS8."

"Oh, I hoped it had a romantic name such as Ocean Warrior."

"I think the day they started making ships that were longer than a football pitch, the romance went out of sailing," said Alex.

"How many crew members did it have?"

"It depended on the cargo," said Alex, "but my guess is twenty-five to thirty."

"So, we're certain that Chidozie Barre was in the Port of Leith in October 1992 and was working on this CB3 Reefer?"

"It's the only ship listed as being there on those specific dates," said Alex, "So, if the story he gave your mother was correct, then the seamen who visited that gift shop came from that ship."

"Eleanor said he was a gentleman," said Lydia. "He wouldn't have lied to her."

Alex hoped Lydia was right.

"Does that mean their next port of call was Rotterdam?" asked Lydia, pointing at the record on-screen.

"Edinburgh to Rotterdam represents at least eighteen hours of sailing time," said Alex, "if my maths is correct."

"Where did it go next?" asked Lydia.

"That will be another search, I'm afraid. There's no guarantee that your Dad stayed with the ship after Rotterdam. He might have switched to another vessel owned by the same company. I vote we contact the company he worked for on that trip and see if he's still registered with them. He's only ten years older than me, at forty-seven. Chidozie should still be in employment somewhere."

"I looked him up on Facebook," said Lydia, "as soon as I discovered his name. Nobody with that name fits the age, place of birth, and description that Eleanor gave."

"Not everyone is glued to their phones on social media, Lydia. Take Gus, for example. His phone is for making calls and sending messages. Your Dad could be another throwback to a bygone age when people talked to one another."

"Perhaps he doesn't want to be found," said Lydia.

"Come on," said Alex, "we knew it would not be easy. We've made progress this morning. Let's take a break, get a bite to eat, and then ask your friend at the Help desk where to find the number for this Greek shipping company."

An hour later, they returned to the Museum to continue the search.

"Does Gus know what we're doing with our brief break?" asked Lydia.

"I didn't tell him our plans," said Alex. "I remember

biting my tongue one day when we were in his car together. I mentioned you were in touch with your birth mother."

"I bet he was complaining about my dress sense again," said Lydia.

"Not that day, if I remember right. He was commending your innate spirit and the fierce way you present yourself to the world. You always give the impression that you're not taking a backward step no matter what."

"That came from my adoptive father," said Lydia. "As soon as I started school in Dundee, the bullies picked on the ginger-haired black girl. He taught me to stand my ground, stare them down, and get my retaliation in first if they looked like they would hit me. I suffered a few detentions for fighting, but the bullying got less. The racist comments never stopped, though, even when I was studying in Glasgow. The streets can be tough up there, unlike the relative peace in the countryside where we work."

Alex thought, not for the first time, that he was a lucky guy. He couldn't imagine getting through the trauma of the last three months without Lydia in his corner. She'd kept him going when he was ready to quit. Now, although he wasn't free of pain in his body, he had the tools to fight that pain without resorting to pills.

This London trip proved he was on the road to recovery. He had left his stick at home, even if the long lunchtime walk they enjoyed was now causing him discomfort.

"Take the weight off that leg," said Lydia. "Sit yourself down while I find that number."

"If you can read my mind, I must watch what I'm thinking," said Alex.

Two minutes later, Lydia returned with a big smile and a slip of paper.

"Got it," she said. "Will you call them, please? I'm scared of what I might find out."

As Alex made the call, Lydia kissed his cheek and headed for the restrooms.

When she returned, Alex sat holding the phone.

"Sit down," he whispered.

"What's up?" asked Lydia.

"Your father continued to work for this Greek shipping company until 2007. He was no ordinary seaman by that time. He had risen to the rank of Chief Mate for the Deck Department."

"Is that an officer?" asked Lydia.

"Yes, I reckon he would be second in command after the Captain. Chidozie was Chief Mate and prioritised the security and safe functioning of the vessel and was responsible for the crew's welfare on board. His responsibilities included the security appliances and the fire prevention equipment. His most important duty was the safe navigation of the ship. Chidozie was an Officer On Watch for the navigational watches between 0400-0800 hrs and 1600-2000 hrs. The Chief Mate constantly oversees the cargo work in the port. It was a responsible position."

"Why did he leave?" asked Lydia.

Alex took Lydia's hands in his.

"He didn't leave. The Greek-owned vessel carried thirty-seven crew and a cargo of fruit and vegetables when it got into trouble in a storm. The vessel had left Darwin on the seventh of May and was sailing out of Manila en route to China. As CB3 Reefer headed across the South China Sea, it floundered, and the crew battled to keep it afloat in terrible storms. Flooding water made conditions slippery underfoot as the crew fought in vain to save the doomed ship. Typhoon Yutu Amang was blowing when the ship sank. The ship's instruments showed it was sailing into high winds of seventy-two knots or eighty-five miles an hour. The Captain sent a distress call to the Philippine Coast Guard and a general mayday for any nearby vessels to come to their aid. Rescuers in an aircraft and four boats and divers searched for survivors. They found a bundle of orange rope and a life jacket. There was no sign of the cargo ship. When they returned to Manila, they received news that a passing freighter had battled violent, rolling waves to reach the spot where the distress signal originated. They found twelve survivors wearing life jackets and floating in rafts."

"Was my father among the survivors?" asked Lydia.

"He was," said Alex, "but the company spokesman told me that after that experience, Chidozie never went to sea again. At least not with their company. The freighter ferried the survivors to Da Nang, Vietnam, where eight spent the night in the hospital. The walking wounded, such as your father, could travel wherever they wished. After the twenty-third of May 2007, the Greek owners don't know where your father went."

"What do we do now?" asked Lydia.

"Let's get back to the hotel, have a night out in London tonight, and then drive home. We confirmed your father was still alive after that tragedy. Twenty-five crew members lost their lives that day."

"I agree; we need a fresh approach. Did Chidozie leave Da Nang right away? Perhaps he returned to Yaba, in Nigeria, to his family home. Hark at me. I'm assuming he had a family home. What made him go to sea in the first place? Where has he been between 2007 and today? Where do you want to go for your holidays this year?"

"If I could get back on a motorcycle, I'd choose Route 66. I've ticked off most of the European trips I wanted to make. But, given that I would have to travel by car once we got to Lagos, I'd be driving if we did go. You're a nightmare on English roads. Heaven knows what they would make of you over there."

Alex and Lydia returned to Chippenham late on Friday morning. Lydia felt it had been a case of two steps forward and three steps back. Alex convinced her that the opposite applied. They had made progress.

Alex drove to his place on Sunday afternoon. He needed to get things together, ready for his return to work. The CRT night out at the Waggon & Horses had reassured him that Gus and the others would be happy to see him. Any awkwardness would go quickly, probably with a quip from Neil Davis.

As he punished himself with an extra dose of physio to make up for the time off in the capital, Alex thought of what lay ahead for Lydia. There were so many possibilities for what happened next to Chidozie Barre. For a man who had been at sea for eighteen years, what career on land would attract him?

Lydia was downhearted when he left her today. Alex thought she should realise they had learned one more important thing over the past two days. Chi-Chi Barre, the junior rating who stole Eleanor's heart, had battled his way to the senior Merchant Navy position of Chief Mate. She needn't look further to explain why she was such a tough cookie. In the toughest of environments, her father had climbed almost to the top of the pole.

Silent Terror: Chapter One

The life and times of Ursula Wakeley 1935-2013

People instinctively recoiled when she called herself a spinster.

But she used the word intentionally and happily because Ursula Wakeley believed such people defined spinsters as often weird, complex, strange beings. She had spent many idle hours in the library in her home town of Mere, defining her version of the modern spinster. One Urban Dictionary entry on *spinster* redefined the term as a woman who can stand independently and doesn't need a man for her life.

"We are living in the age of the single woman," Ursula told a younger colleague.

The shallow smile Ursula received was a typical response from the unenlightened.

Ursula believed she shouldn't get defined by the lack of a husband or children. Those who sneered when she celebrated that she was unmarried and childless either considered her invisible or despised her.

229

Ursula was born in 1935, the second child of Gideon and Elspeth Wakeley. Gideon was a God-fearing man who toiled as an agricultural labourer until the day he died. Her father never saw the Harvest Festival at the Methodist Church in late September 1966. He dropped dead in the fields a mile from his home on the first day of the month. He was fifty-six. His widow, Elspeth, was two years his junior and needed Ursula at home.

Arthur Wakeley, Assistant Manager at Lloyd's Bank in the town, told Ursula there was nothing to discuss. However, she must give up her job as a librarian and stay home to care for their mother. Arthur was two years older than Ursula and married to Glenda, a former bank cashier. They lived in the town with their two children.

Ursula protested. Why did it fall on her shoulders? She, too, had attended the small school in the town, just like her brother. From the age of eleven, they had made the daily bus trip from Mere, a tiny town on the edge of Salisbury Plain in Wiltshire, to the Gillingham School, across the county border in Dorset. Arthur and Ursula left on the same day in July 1952. Her exam results in the newly introduced O-Levels were two grades higher than anything Arthur had achieved at sixteen. Her brother studied three subjects at A-Level and scraped a bare pass in Maths, History, and Geography.

Ursula would have loved to stay on for two further years like her brother. She even dreamed of going to University, but Gideon and Elspeth were adamant. They needed their youngest daughter to bring in a weekly wage to boost the family budget.

"Arthur will marry, and his banking career will take him away from the town," said Gideon. "Your place is here with your mother and me until you marry."

Ursula had started at the library on Barton Lane in September 1952. The fourteen years she spent surrounded by books was the happiest period of her life. She reluctantly handed in her notice within a week of her father's funeral.

Arthur had indeed married and moved to different towns with the bank. Ursula found it ironic that Glenda Simpkins, her best friend at Gillingham school, was the girl Arthur married. When they walked through the school gates together for the final time, Glenda raved about the letter she had received that morning. She had a job offer at the bank as a junior clerk.

"I'll be working with that brother of yours," she grinned. "He's going places, and if I can turn his head, I'll see the country with him. I don't want to stay in this back-water of a place forever."

Glenda never travelled far. She had two children in the first four years of marriage and never returned to work after leaving to await the arrival of Matthew. By the time Samantha arrived, Arthur's career had stalled. He would climb no higher than an Assistant Manager. Rather than move to a manager's position in Salisbury, Dorchester, or further afield, Glenda discovered they were returning to Mere for Arthur to while away the days until he could retire.

No wonder he insisted that I quit my job to look after our mother, thought Ursula. He was bitter. Arthur resented the pleasure I got from my job at the library. And he still hadn't forgiven her for outshining him at school.

Elspeth Wakeley was not the easiest person to live with, but Ursula knuckled down to the task. The years passed, and although she still harboured hopes of a man showing an interest in her at thirty-one, it became apparent that nobody wanted to take on two women.

Caring for an elderly relative can be arduous, and Elspeth made things as difficult as possible. Ursula had never noticed how much of a hypochondriac her mother was until after her father's death. There was always something. It was a release when Elspeth succumbed to a particularly virulent bout of influenza that gripped the country between October and Christmas 1996. Ursula's prison sentence was complete.

"Thirty years," she said to Arthur and Glenda on Boxing Day. "Even the Great Train Robbers never served that long a sentence."

To Arthur's great surprise, the sixty-one-year-old Ursula approached the library to explore the possibility of taking up her old position. They were happy to have her back. After all, she was a familiar face and had visited the library at least twice a week since she quit. When the staff had asked after Elspeth, Ursula told them this was her place of sanctuary. Somewhere she could escape from her mother, if only for an hour.

Retirement at sixty-five wasn't compulsory in more enlightened times, and Ursula continued to patrol the bookshelves of her beloved library until she reached seventy-five. She often remarked that she would have done the job for nothing.

Times had changed. Ursula realised that the people who visited the library were nowhere near as well-behaved as those she remembered from her earlier years.

"There are signs everywhere," she would say. "Why do they bother coming here if they can't read? Quiet means just that. Either don't talk or whisper. I've lost count of the number of times I've had to reprimand people. As for the unemployed, or the retirees, they wander indoors for warmth and to read the daily newspaper. They can't afford to buy one because they need every penny in their pocket when the pubs open. I needn't look at the clock on the wall. I know when it's eleven o'clock because there's a queue at the door to get out. It's worse in the afternoons. They troop back in, smelling of drink, and often something far worse."

When Ursula retired, she didn't stop visiting the library. She still popped in whenever she was in town. Old habits are hard to break. Noisy schoolchildren and drunken senior citizens with flatulence continued to feel the sharp edge of her tongue.

Ursula was an avid reader, and the things that occupied her mind while she sat in silence poring over her work wouldn't have been what most observers would expect.

Wednesday, 16 January 2013

As she relaxed in her father's chair by the fireside, Ursula let her mind drift back over the benefits of living alone.

There was a special magic in sitting in the kitchen in the morning, reading or waiting for the bread to bake. She could lounge on the sofa, checking the headlines on the daily newspaper in the middle of the afternoon if she wished. Knick-knacks surrounded her on an evening such as this. Items that had belonged to her parents or that Ursula collected on recent holidays abroad.

Ursula knew with absolute certainty that no one could tell her she had too many books, several unnecessary scatter cushions, and that the television was far too loud. Why? Because she lived alone and she loved it. The trick had been to arrange her life the way she wanted it after her mother died.

"I don't see any biological reason women should marry or have children," she'd told Glenda, her sister-in-law, last weekend. "I was reading an article in the library just this week that suggested men and women were never meant to stay together for a long time. They should procreate and leave. No wonder so many modern marriages fail. Once any children can survive alone, there's no point continuing the relationship. Look at you and Arthur. You've spent the last thirty years hating the sight of one another. Where are you off tomorrow? Visiting your son, I suppose? Matthew's fifty-seven, married, with two children and three grandchildren. He doesn't need you. What did you do after you fell pregnant with him? You stopped working and became a full-time housewife. You loved that job and could have gone on to higher positions at that bank. If a young woman today wants to focus on a career, it's simpler to remain single. Look at your Samantha. You never see her from one Christmas to the next. She's flying around the world on long-haul flights as an air stewardess. Samantha was sensible enough to realise she didn't need a man to validate her existence."

Glenda gave the same response as everyone else of her generation. It's what you did back then.

Being single all these years had given Ursula valuable time to pursue her pet projects and be her own person. She was happy she'd used her time alone to figure out who she was.

Ursula turned the volume up another notch on the TV. Her neighbours were one hundred yards in either direction; they wouldn't hear. It's odd how these things creep up on you as you get older. She could spot a loud whisper in the library when she returned to work after her mother passed.

The year before she retired, Ursula noticed subtle

changes in her hearing. Colleagues would nudge her arm to catch her attention. She would apologise and claim she was engrossed in an article or the blurb of a new book and hadn't heard them speak. Then, a year later, she watched her colleagues' lips to confirm what she thought they were saying. In the past three years, things had gotten worse.

Because the bungalow stood on a quiet road, surrounded by trees on three sides, Ursula no longer followed her parents' custom of drawing every curtain in the house the minute the sun set. Why bother? There was never anyone in the open fields beyond the trees after sundown. The occasional car passed the bungalow on winter evenings, but nobody came calling.

Ursula enjoyed seeing the moon and stars through her bedroom window when she went to bed and the sun when it woke her in the mornings. It was another mechanism she had adopted to celebrate her single life. If she undressed in the dark before slipping into bed or wandered naked to the bathroom in the morning, who's business was it but her own?

Ursula had established a strict rota for visitors that matched her daily calendar. Don Hillier arrived on Tuesday and Thursday at ten o'clock. Don was ten years younger than Ursula and hadn't adjusted to retirement. He needed to keep busy. Ursula paid him to tend to the garden and those annoying little jobs that an ageing property accumulates.

Don had been her handyman for three years but had never once stepped inside the bungalow. His employment was strictly for outdoor maintenance. He offered to fix a dripping tap or move heavy furniture to let Ursula spring-clean the place. All offers received a polite but firm refusal. Ursula insisted she could manage what needed doing. Don held his tongue. Everything stayed as it had been when he arrived to mow the lawn for the first time.

Ursula visited the library on Monday, Wednesday, and Friday morning. Saturday was the one day in the week when she spent more than the minimum amount of time away from the bungalow. Her first job in the morning was to get her baking done for the coming week. Then she went into town to do her weekly shop at the supermarket. She was strict about delivery time. After shopping, she had lunch at the corner café before spending two hours in her beloved library. She arrived home at four fifteen precisely to await the supermarket delivery van at half-past four.

One might have expected Ursula to treat Sundays differently from her parents. But, instead, she attended the Mere Methodist Church services at ten-thirty and seven o'clock in the evening.

On this particular Wednesday evening, Ursula sat closer to the roaring log fire. Don Hillier had sawn plenty of wood to keep her warm during this cold snap, but the outside temperature hadn't risen above freezing all day. The trip to town to visit the library had been an adventure. Almost every step she'd taken on the pavements risked a fall. At seventy-eight, Ursula knew how dangerous that could prove.

She was thankful to be safe indoors and could no longer hear the wind rattling the loose guttering Don was due to fix tomorrow. She glanced at the television. How long had it been since the programme she'd been watching had finished? Her mind had wandered. Was there anything worth staying up to watch? Ursula turned off the TV, got up from her chair and went into the kitchen. It was time for a cup of hot chocolate to take across the hallway to her bedroom. Then, standing at the sink to fill the kettle, she saw something move in the back garden.

Was that someone standing under the apple tree in the far corner? She couldn't make out a face from this distance. What did they think they were doing? Ursula hesitated. Was it her imagination? The trees were twenty yards away, and the movement had ceased. It must have been a trick of the moonlight. The kettle soon boiled, and Ursula carried the cup in both hands back into the living room.

The cup of hot chocolate hit the floor, and Ursula screamed. There was a face at the front window. The image was familiar. The person wore one of those Scream masks that were everywhere at Halloween. A second later, the face disappeared. Ursula scurried to the window as best she could. It must be children, she thought. The little devils wanted to scare her. Well, perhaps it was time to draw the curtains after all.

As she stretched to draw the curtains together, the masked face sprang up from beneath the window. Ursula screamed again and staggered backwards.

She cursed the silence.

Ursula hadn't closed the curtains completely. She stared at the gap, praying the person had run away. Maybe they were next door now, terrorising her neighbour, Beryl Giddings. This silly game had gone on long enough. She should call the police.

A shape darted past the window, heading for her front door.

The landline was in the hallway. Ursula moved towards the door.

She hadn't heard the back door opening. All she could think about was the person wearing the Scream mask staring at her through the gap in the curtain.

Something alerted Ursula to the danger behind her.

Unfortunately, she turned too late as she felt a crushing blow to the back of her head and fell to the floor.

Ursula Wakeley didn't see the person behind her run to the door to let in their accomplice. Her attackers studied the huddled shape on the floor. The old witch was still breathing. Okay, now it was time to have fun.

Silent Terror: Chapter Two

Thursday, 17 January 2013

Don Hillier pushed his bicycle along Shaftesbury Road at the appointed time. He passed the gateway to Two Counties Farm as he gingerly made his way towards Ursula Wakeley's bungalow.

He thought it odd that Ursula hadn't drawn her curtains at this time of day.

Don had set off from home earlier than usual. The gritters were out last night, and the major roads were passable for traffic. Once you ventured onto the side streets and lanes, however, then you were asking for trouble. Don felt safer with his bicycle to lean on as he slipped and skated the last part of his journey. There was a weak sun this morning. However, the forecast was improving, and the temperature was in the low digits.

He expected to see Ursula at the front door, ready to issue new instructions, but there was no sign. He rested his bicycle against the front porch, stepped up and rang the doorbell. She couldn't have gone into town, could she? It was Thursday.

Don decided to get on with repairing the guttering. He walked to the garden shed at the side of the bungalow and carried the short ladder to the front. He rested it against the top row of bricks, and after checking the foot of the ladder was secure, he climbed.

The gap in the curtains didn't allow the handyman to see much of the living room. Two things looked strange to Don. When did he last see these curtains drawn, anyway? He couldn't recall, and there was a stain on the carpet by the kitchen door. He didn't believe Ursula would leave it that way for so long. As his eyes grew accustomed to the dark interior of the house, he saw that the back door was open.

Ursula was nowhere to be seen in the back garden when he fetched the ladder from the shed. He would have heard her. There was something amiss. Don didn't possess a mobile phone, so he walked to Charles Marshall's next door. He knew the older man was up, as he'd seen Charles putting something in the recycling bin when he came along the road. It was probably another empty gin bottle.

He tapped on the front door.

"Don, what can I do for you?" asked Charles.

"Ursula isn't answering her door, Charles. The back door's open. I'm afraid something might have happened to her."

"Do you want me to ring for an ambulance? Maybe Ursula went outside in the dark last night and slipped on the ice?"

Don knew Ursula's reaction if they made a mountain out of a molehill.

"Do you have her brother Arthur's number?" asked Don.

"It'll be in the directory. Let me give Arthur a call. Come on in out of the cold, Don."

Ten minutes later, Arthur Wakeley drove past the Marshall residence and swung into the driveway of his sister's bungalow. It was clear to Don Hillier that Arthur was not best pleased.

"I'll get along there and explain," said Don, "many thanks for your help, Charles."

"No problem. Let me know, won't you? She can be a funny old stick but a good neighbour."

"You mean she never bothers you," laughed Don.

"Ha, exactly," said Charles.

When Don reached the entrance to the driveway, Arthur was already inside the bungalow. Don wasn't surprised that Arthur had a key. He stood outside on the porch and waited.

Arthur reappeared.

"You're as white as a sheet, Arthur," said Don. "Is everything alright?"

"I need to phone the police," said Arthur, "someone broke in last night and…."

"Not dead," said Don, "surely you can't mean someone killed Ursula?"

Arthur shook his head.

"I can't go back in there," he said, "what he did to her. He must be an animal."

Local newspapers carried various reports of the spinster's murder throughout the police investigation.

'Miss Ursula Wakeley was seventy-eight years old when someone stabbed her to death in her bungalow on Shaftesbury Road, Mere. Her elder brother Arthur found the body. Don Hillier, a handyman expecting to work for the retired librarian, raised the alarm.'

'Ursula Wakeley's death prompted the largest police investigation in the town's history, and, despite the attraction of a sizeable reward, they never identified her killer. Police believed the killer lived in the local area and was shielded by a friend or family member after the murder.'

'The killer broke into the rear of her home to rob Miss Wakeley and repeatedly stabbed her when she challenged him. The killer removed a quantity of jewellery from one bedroom. Police estimated the value of the haul at only two thousand pounds.'

Grab your copy...
vinci-books.com/silentterror